Wild Kat McCrumble

Other books by Margaret Ryan:

Kat McCrumble
Simply Kat McCrumble

Operation Boyfriend
Operation Handsome
Operation Wedding

And for younger readers:

HOVER BOY:
1. Fizzy Feet
2. Beat the Bully
3. Missing Moggy Mystery

THE CANTERBURY TALES:
1. The Big Sister's Tale
2. The Little Brother's Tale
3. The Little Sister's Tale

To Susie
Happy Reading,
Margaret Ryan

Wild KAT McCRUMBLE

MARGARET RYAN

Hodder
Children's
Books

A division of Hodder Headline Limited

To Tia with love

Text copyright © 2005 Margaret Ryan
Illustrations copyright © 2005 Jan McCafferty
First published in 2005 by Hodder Children's Books

The rights of Margaret Ryan and Jan McCafferty
to be identified as the Author and Illustrator of the work
respectively have been asserted by them in accordance
with the Copyright, Designs and Patents Act 1988.

2 4 6 8 10 9 7 5 3 1

A Catalogue record for this book is available
from the British Library

ISBN 0 340 88402 9

Typeset in Baskerville by Avon DataSet Ltd,
Bidford-on-Avon, Warwickshire

Printed and bound in Great Britain by
Bookmarque Ltd, Croydon, Surrey

The paper and board used in this paperback by Hodder
Children's Books are natural recyclable products made from
wood grown in sustainable forests. The manufacturing
processes conform to the environmental regulations
of the country of origin.

Hodder Children's Books
A division of Hodder Headline Limited
338 Euston Road
London NW1 3BH

Scottish for Beginners

Auchtertuie: the village where I live. I know it looks a little like a giant sneeze, but you can say it. Honest. Try . . . OCH-TER-2-Y. See. Easy.

Bannocks: round flat cakes made with oatmeal and flour. Yummy.

Dry stane dykes: Dry stone walls. Kind of like vertical jigsaws. You could try making one, but mind your toes.

Eightsome reel and Strip the Willow: fast and furious Scottish country dances. Noisy and exhausting. You'd like them.

Eilidh: pronounced 'AYLAY' and Gaelic for Helen. If you're called Helen you could be really annoying and change your name to Eilidh.

Ne'er cast a clout till May be oot: wrap up warmly, you only THINK it's summertime. Saying beloved of Scottish grannies who would sew you into your anorak if they could.

Plaid: pronounced 'PLAD'. Rectangular length of woollen cloth usually in tartan. Now only worn as ceremonial dress by people in pipe bands, and daft folk at weddings.

Tam o' Shanter: a flat crowned cap. You wouldn't be seen dead in one.

Wheech: to whisk away. As in, 'My mum wheeched away the chocolate biscuits and I was only on my fifth'.

Chapter 1

Hi, I'm Kat. That's me on the front cover looking sophisticated and gorgeous. I wish! Sometimes I wish I could be beautiful and elegant like the models in the magazines, but with my red hair and freckles, and a wardrobe full of scruffy jeans, that could be tricky. Other times I wish that my name was short for something more exotic than Katriona. Katya perhaps, or Katinka. But then Katya Mhairi McCrumble might sound a bit odd, and the Nisbet boys from the hill farm would be sure to turn Katinka into Kastinka. Safer just to be Kat.

What I never wish for is to live anywhere else. I love Auchtertuie. It's a village on the west coast of Scotland, near Fort William, and just north of the

Great Glen. When I was little I asked my dad, 'If there's a Great Glen, does that mean there's also a Not So Great Glen, or even a Pretty Horrible Glen?'

But he said, 'No, Kat, the name Great Glen comes from the Gaelic Glen More. "More" meaning "great" in English.'

He's full of odd bits of information like that, my dad. He says he just knows a little about a lot of things, but he knows a lot about the history of the McCrumble family. He talks to me about it sometimes. Goes on a bit, actually. I do my best to listen intelligently, but when we get on to the great-great-aunts and uncles, my eyes glaze over and I start to wonder what Kirsty's cooking for lunch. I expect I'll be more interested in the family history when I'm older. Much older.

Kirsty's much older than I am, and a McCrumble too, and she doesn't know all about the family history yet. But she does know all about cooking. She's our cook at the Crumbling Arms inn. That's where I live with my dad, Hector. It's a two-storey white building on the shore road in Auchtertuie. The inn has the high Ben Bracken at its back and the deep Loch Bracken at its front. It's a bit like the filling in a bracken sandwich. Did you know that in the olden days people used to pile bracken up and use it as a mattress to sleep on? So Dad says. Funny how he can remember things like that, but often doesn't know what day of the week it is. But Kirsty tries to keep him right. So does Morag. She's our postie and has the 'second sight'. She foretells things; like what's in your mail, or who's won money on the lottery, or even who's going on an unexpected holiday. Though sometimes she doesn't get it quite right. She recently told old Mrs Corbet she was going on an unexpected trip, and Mrs Corbet went looking for her suitcase and tripped over Solly, her cat. We looked after him while she was in the cottage hospital with her broken leg. Morag went to see her every day and took her lots of flowers.

Dad doesn't believe in the 'second sight' and thinks Morag is mad. She is. Mad about him. Fancies him like crazy. But Dad is oblivious. Just doesn't notice. Now, if she were a great-great-auntie Morag McCrumble in a long black frock and black button-up boots, he might pay her a bit more attention. As it is, his attention is taken up with running the Crumbling Arms and the wildlife sanctuary we have at the back of the inn. We take care of any distressed animals or birds that are brought to us, and whenever possible, release them back into the wild.

All our pens and runs are a bit ramshackle at the

moment, as Dad and Donald, our handyman, make them themselves. One day we hope to have enough money to build things properly, but Donald, who's a druid, and loves all trees, plants and animals, says, 'So long as the animals are happy, Kat, that's all that matters. They don't mind if they don't have state-of-the-art accommodation.'

I'm sure he's right. With Donald's help, and Kirsty's and Morag's, Dad and I manage to keep the inn and the sanctuary going.

No thanks to another McCrumble, Callum McCrumble, who owns the luxury hotel and the big estate which stretches out for miles behind the Crumbling Arms. For some time now, Callum's been trying to close down the Crumbling Arms and acquire the inn for himself. With the help of Ron Jackson, his horrible gamekeeper, he has played a few really nasty tricks on us, but we have managed to win through. So far. But we have to keep an eagle eye on him. He might be a McCrumble, but he's from the rotten branch of the family tree. I'll tell you more about that later. I do know a little about McCrumble family history.

Meantime, things were going along fairly quietly at the Crumbling Arms. We had plenty of guests, both human and animal, and we hoped that Callum had given up on the dirty tricks for a while, and that we'd get some peace. But we hoped in vain. Just when we thought Callum McCrumble had crawled back into his black hole and pulled the lid shut, up popped another McCrumble. Just as bad.

Chapter 2

Perhaps I should tell you a bit more about the Crumbling Arms, in case you might want to visit one day.

If you are a seriously up-market person, or have just won the lottery, or are a famous film star who wants a five-star holiday with luxury swimming pool, jacuzzi and hot and cold running room service, don't come to the Crumbling Arms. If you want amusement arcades, flashing lights, and greasy hamburgers and chips, don't come to the Crumbling Arms. If you want a hotel manager with a posh suit and an even posher accent, don't come to the Crumbling Arms.

BUT . . .

If you want great food, loads of animals and ME (and sometimes my best friend, Tina Morrison), then DO come to the Crumbling Arms. You will be very welcome. But you must be prepared to share your holiday with donkeys, dogs, cats, badgers and . . . the occasional ghost . . .

Did I mention we have a ghost? He's called Old Hamish and comes from the good branch of the family tree. In fact, he's as far back as we can trace the McCrumbles. There were twin brothers then, Hamish and Callum, and they lived in McCrumble Castle, and owned the land, which is now the estate. Hamish was the nice guy. He looked after the land and the people on it, and kept the castle in good order. Callum was the prat. He spent all the money, then vanished leaving Hamish to cope with his debts. Hamish did his best. He wanted to keep the family's good name. But paying off the debts left no money for the upkeep of the castle, which fell into disrepair, then ruin. Old Hamish died, still awaiting the safe return of his twin brother.

Years later another McCrumble built the Crumbling Arms inn, using the stones from the old McCrumble castle. What he didn't know was that Old Hamish's ghost came too. He lives (?) with us in the Crumbling Arms. But don't be alarmed, he's not really scary. Just looks a bit odd with his long grey hair and his old McCrumble tartan kilt and plaid. But his face has a kindly expression and he means no harm. He doesn't appear to everyone, though. He appears to me when he knows there's trouble brewing, and he does what he can to help. That's what I think anyway. Dad thinks I'm as mad as Morag. But he hasn't met Old Hamish. But you might. Who knows?

I definitely know you'll meet the Border collies, Millie and Max. At least, you'll meet Millie; you'll probably fall over Max. He gets everywhere he shouldn't, including on top of my duvet with his muddiest paws. You should hear Kirsty yell when she finds out. No, on second thoughts, you probably shouldn't. It's not a pretty sound. Max is Millie's son, and a great trial to her. I don't think she can believe how such a sane, sensible parent like herself could have raised such a lunatic offspring as Max. But then sometimes I think my dad feels the same way about me!

But I'm not mad. I just GET mad. Especially where animal cruelty is concerned. One of our donkeys, Donk, is a rescue donkey, who had been terribly badly treated by his previous owner, and our cat, Samantha, had just been abandoned. Fortunately she was left near us, so we were able to take her in and look after her. Not that SHE thinks we did that. She thinks she's doing us a favour just by living with us, high and mighty creature that she is. She shares her cat food with Flip. He's our semi-tame badger who flips open the cat flap and comes into the kitchen most evenings to have his dinner. Chicken liver's his favourite. He's my special friend, and together with Tina and the other animals we have shared in some pretty hairy adventures.

Now we were about to share in some more.

Chapter 3

The day of our adventure began like any other. Down in the kitchen Dad burnt the guests' toast, the smoke alarm went off, and I hurtled downstairs to help with the breakfasts. Kirsty doesn't come in till ten o'clock, so I try to give Dad a hand whenever I can. I can grill a mean sausage, and fry an egg to perfection, so long as you want it sunny side up. I try to be sunny in the mornings too, but it's not easy. Dad says when you run an inn, you always have to be really friendly and polite to the guests. I can do friendly and polite, it's awake I have difficulty with some mornings. But at least I can remember that the porridge goes in the pot and the bacon under the grill, unlike

Dad, who's even been known to attempt to fry cornflakes.

We had three guests that morning; three brothers who come to Auchtertuie every year to climb Ben Bracken. And they're always kidding around.

'Ah, it's the lovely Kat,' said Eric, the eldest, when I appeared in the dining room with their toast. 'And what culinary delights have you brought us this morning?'

I grinned. I didn't have to be too polite with this lot.

'A speciality of the house,' I said. 'Six slices of carbon-coated bread which I personally scraped for you.'

'Excellent. My favourite. And to follow?'

'Porridge à la lumpy bits and cremated bacon.'

'On the same plate, I hope,' said Thomas, the middle one.

'But of course,' I replied. 'Ecologically sound. Saves on the washing up, but mind your teeth on the crispy bits.'

'No problem,' said Neil, the youngest. 'I always take mine out to chew.'

'Kirsty does that too, but only when she needs them to crimp the pastries for afternoon tea,' I replied. It was as well Kirsty wasn't around to hear me, or I would have been toast. Then I left the brothers to tuck into their delicious (honest) breakfast.

That's what I like about running an inn, you get to meet so many different people.

The climbers finished their breakfast, collected their rucksacks and set off up the Ben. I was just heading back into the dining room to clear away the dishes when a strange sight brought me to a skidding halt. A boat had entered the loch and was mooring not far off shore. Now there's nothing strange about a boat on the loch, we get them all the time; fishing boats, sailing boats, speedboats, rowing-boats. But never one the size of a small town before, never one with the name 'McCrumble' written in gold letters on its stern, and never one painted entirely and luminously in the colours of the McCrumble tartan. Even the flags fluttering in the breeze were McCrumble tartan.

'Dad,' I yelled. 'Come and see this.'

Dad, followed by Millie and Max, joined me at the front door. Dad grinned.

'Just call it a hunch,' he said, 'but it looks like we have another McCrumble come to visit the old homeland.'

We left the inn and crossed the shore road to have a closer look.

A small crowd had gathered by the lochside,

including Jinty McCrumble from the bakery. She takes her hens over to the lochside every morning and leaves them there to wander till night-time.

'Much better for them than being cooped up all day,' she says.

The hens look really colourful as they peck about amongst the pebbles. The tourists' children love them and often have their photographs taken holding one. And the hens are no trouble at all, although one did lose her way once and visited Evie McCrumble in the tiny post office. Apparently she left a small deposit that had nothing to do with a savings account. But Evie didn't mind, Jinty gave her some free eggs.

'Did you ever see the likes of that in all your life?' Jinty started to say to us, waving a dismissive hand towards the tartan boat, when her words were drowned out by the tinny sound of Scottish country dance emanating from the bow. Some people in the crowd laughed, and started to do a little impromptu dance, linking arms and doing a figure of eight on the small patch of gravelly sand. Max thought that looked like fun and joined in, weaving in and out among the legs of the dancers. Then the dancers stopped and watched as a rowing-boat was lowered from the stern, and a member of the crew climbed down into it. He sat amidships and picked up the oars. He was followed by a piper dressed in McCrumble tartan trousers and a white, loose-fitting shirt. When he was settled in the bow, a row of sailors, also in McCrumble tartan trews, appeared on deck and saluted as a further figure appeared. This one wore full McCrumble Highland regalia, including a long plaid thrown over his shoulder. It appeared to be held by a large silver brooch which glinted in the morning sunlight, as did the many silver buttons on his Bonnie Prince Charlie black jacket. But perhaps the most striking thing about his outfit was the enormous black velvet Tam o' Shanter, adorned with grouse feathers, that he wore on top of his long grey hair. Then, suddenly, while we were all gawping – Auchtertuie had never seen anything like this before – the country dance music stopped and the piper in the rowing-boat took over. He stood up, a trifle unsteadily, and began to play 'Scotland the Brave', and the McCrumble in the fancy hat was ceremoniously rowed towards the shore.

Everyone looked at one another. What was this? Some kind of publicity stunt? Was this to advertise something? Was this some bigwig, come to stay at the big hotel, announcing his arrival?

We watched as the rowing-boat crunched ashore, the piper stopped playing, and the Highlander in the stern stepped out on to the sand. That's when we saw the thickness of his tartan calves and the enormous silver buckles on his big black shoes. Last time I'd seen buckles that big they'd been on the shoes of the giant in the Jack and the Beanstalk Christmas pantomime in Fort William. This giant strode towards us – not easy on sand – and held up an imperious, beringed hand for silence.

Everyone quietened down, curious to hear what he had to say. Max was curious too. He sat on the sand beside this strange figure and hung out his pink tongue. One of the few things he does really well.

'Is there one among you who has the Crumbling Arms inn?' asked the stranger in a booming voice with a Russian-style accent.

Dad looked mildly surprised. 'I'm Hector McCrumble. I own the Crumbling Arms. Have you come to Scotland on a visit?'

'Visit? No. I have come to stay,' said the stranger. 'I am Vladimir McCrumble. I have come to Scotland to claim my birthright. I am the rightful chief of the Clan McCrumble. Here is a copy of the document that proves it. The Crumbling Arms is no longer yours, Hector McCrumble. The Crumbling Arms is mine.'

Whaaaat!!!???

Chapter 4

Everyone gasped. Especially me.

'Is this some kind of a joke?' frowned Dad, examining the official-looking document.

'If it is, it's not very funny,' I said. 'You should sack your scriptwriter.'

'Och, it'll be some advertising stunt, Kat.' Jinty was dismissive. 'What are you selling, Vladimir? If it's porridge oats, I already get mine from the Co-op.'

Plaid-clad Vlad pulled himself up to his not inconsiderable height.

'I am a chief,' he proclaimed. 'I sell nothing. Who are you?'

'Oh, I'm a chief too,' said Jinty. 'Chief bun maker

at the bakery, and I haven't got time for any more of this nonsense. I have scones and pies to sell.' And she turned on her heel and left.

Meantime Dad's frown had deepened.

'You've obviously done some family research, Vladimir,' he said. 'But you must have got it wrong.'

'So you say, as I knew you would.' Vladimir wasn't a bit put out. 'So, I will see you in court, Hector McCrumble. The lawyers will argue the case. I am chieftain. I do not argue. I win. But for now you have my permission to stay in the Crumbling Arms and run it as best you can. Naturally I will change everything when you leave and I take up residence. Now that is all for the moment, I think. I must go. I am very busy man. Good day to you.'

Good day? He had to be joking. For once I was too astonished to say anything. My jaw had dropped and was still falling.

Vladimir strode back to his rowing-boat, a curious Max sniffing at his heels. He turned and gave the little crowd a royal wave, then lifted one tartan leg to climb aboard. That was when Max, fascinated by the fringes on Vlad's plaid, pounced. He caught them in his teeth and gave them a good yank. The so-called chieftain gave a very undignified yell and fell backwards on to the sand. His hat and his hair fell off to reveal a billiard ball head. Everyone laughed. Max, pleased with himself, wagged his tail and picked up the hat and wig and brought them over to Dad, dropping them on the sand at his feet.

'Sorry,' Dad smiled, as he picked them up and handed them back to their owner.

'Do not worry, you will be,' muttered Vladimir and, with as much dignity as he could muster, put his hat and his hair back on and climbed into the rowing-boat. The piper started to play again.

'Shut up,' yelled Vladimir, and, his face stiff with annoyance, he was rowed back in silence to his big boat.

The crowd gave a small cheer and I finally found my voice. 'This IS a joke, Dad, isn't it? There is no way that guy can be for real. Perhaps there's a hidden camera somewhere and we'll all end up on the telly.' And I looked around hopefully. But the only cameras were those belonging to the tourists who were taking photos of Vlad and the tartan-painted boat. They'd probably go home and tell their friends tales of the strange people who live in Scotland. But Vladimir McCrumble, if that was his real name, was more than just strange.

'Perhaps he's a wacko, Dad,' I said. 'You know, two dips short of a sherbert. Missing most of his marbles. A serious loony, in fact.'

Dad shook his head. 'This document shows that

work has been done on his ancestry. Seems to show that it might be as good as ours. Seems to show that he may have a legitimate claim to the Crumbling Arms. I need to have it checked out right away. This could just be serious, Kat.'

I cast a baleful glance at Vladimir, whose tartan-clad legs were now ascending the iron ladder of the floating *McCrumble*.

'He can't be for real,' I said. 'Nobody paints their boat tartan and sails into Auchtertuie claiming to be clan chief. It's just not normal.'

But then, life in Auchtertuie was seldom normal, and after that, life was even less normal than normal. If you see what I mean.

Chapter 5

I called the dogs to heel, and Dad and I crossed the street and went back into the inn. Dad was deep in thought. I wore a deep frown. Max's nose was deep in the turn-ups of my jeans, searching for crumbs. That dog is a walking stomach. Two minutes later Kirsty arrived, laden with carrier bags. She'd been to collect the day's supplies from James Ross, the butcher. Max immediately abandoned my turn-ups and headed for the shopping. But Kirsty was ready for him. To his great disgust, she wheeched the meat straight into the fridge as she always does. Max was left looking forlorn. He gave a deep sigh at the unfairness of it all and settled down to guard the fridge. He would have to watch it carefully now.

If the tiniest morsel should escape from its cavernous depths, he'd be ready. Millie sighed too. She slid her nose down on to her front paws and lay quietly, watching Max.

'Have you seen that monstrosity out there in the loch?' sniffed Kirsty, when all the shopping was safely stowed away. 'Who in their right mind would paint their boat tartan?'

'Vladimir McCrumble,' I said. 'So-called chieftain of the Clan McCrumble.'

'You're joking,' said Kirsty, and laughed as she put the kettle on. 'We get them all here, right enough.'

But she wasn't laughing when Dad showed her the document Vladimir had handed to him, and she certainly wasn't laughing when he told her the story.

Kirsty examined the family tree in disbelief. 'Either this is a bad joke, Hector, or this Vladimir person can't be right in the head,' she said. 'Perhaps the poor soul needs help. Perhaps he shouldn't be allowed out alone. Perhaps we should alert Doctor Walls.'

'Unfortunately, I think Vladimir is perfectly serious,' said Dad. 'And, at first glance, this family tree seems authentic enough. I must go upstairs and check it out right away.'

The words were hardly out of his mouth when the back door opened and Morag came in with the post. Her eyes were bright with excitement.

'I was just driving down the lochside when I saw the big boat,' she said. 'Did you ever see the likes of that in all your life? What's it all about? Have you seen any cameras? Maybe someone's making a funny advert or even a film. I've always wanted to be in films. I wonder if they need any extras. A walk-on part as the trusty postie would do, but a bigger part as the glamorous postie with the second sight would be even better.'

'Second sight?' snorted Dad. 'How come you didn't foresee a tartan boat sailing up the loch, then? That's hardly a common occurrence.'

'I can't foretell everything, Hector.' Morag wasn't a bit put out. 'It doesn't work like that.' And she settled down at the kitchen table to have her usual morning cup of tea and scone.

The back door opened again and my friend, Tina, appeared.

'Hi, Kat. Hullo, everyone. Have you seen the . . . ?'

We all nodded. 'Uh-huh.'

'He can't really be the chieftain, can he?' asked Tina.

I told you news travels fast in Auchtertuie.

'Of course not,' I said. 'He's an imposter. He's

just someone out to make a name for himself. He's just someone out to try to make trouble for us.'

I stopped as Morag stiffened and went glassy-eyed. She slipped into one of her trances and her scone slid from her hand. Max gave up guarding the fridge, and shot over and gulped it in one. Kirsty rescued Morag's cup of tea before it too fell to the floor. We lost a lot of cups that way. Morag's eye – the blue one it was, the other one's amber – took on its faraway look.

'I see the Crumbling Arms,' she said in a hollow voice.

No surprise there. We were all sitting in its kitchen.

'I see the Crumbling Arms crumbling.'

No surprise there either. We were all well used to bits of the Crumbling Arms falling off, breaking down or just generally giving up. Donald and Dad spent much of their time trying to patch it up and keep it all together.

'I see trouble ahead.' Morag was going on.

'We know that, Morag,' I sighed. 'You only have to look out of the window to see a whole boat-load of trouble.'

But Morag wasn't listening.

'I see lots of trouble. From all around. Trouble

24

from the sea, trouble from the air. Trouble, trouble everywhere.'

Morag was being quite poetic, but not much help.

Tina looked at me anxiously. 'What do you think it all means, Kat?'

I shook my head and stroked Millie's silky ears. I hadn't a clue, and, the trouble was, I didn't think anyone else had either.

Chapter 6

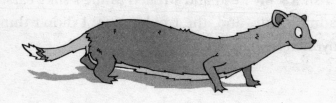

Have you ever noticed how older people sometimes enjoy being glum? Their faces get a solemn, set look and they shake their heads a lot. Then they come out with their special little glum sayings like ... 'It never rains but it pours.' Or 'Mark my words, no good will come of it.' Or the Scottish one, 'Ne'er cast a clout till May be oot,' which probably means something about the may blossom appearing, but Kirsty uses to mean, 'Don't take off your vest or go without your anorak till June, Kat McCrumble, or it's bound to rain, snow, hail and thunder, all at the same time.' She's really fond of saying that to me, especially when I try to skip out to school without my anorak. Only dweebs and dorks wear anoraks to school, and Kirsty doesn't understand that. I know she's just trying to look after me because my mum died when I was little, but even so, a girl has to watch her image, and mine is scruffy, not wimpy. But that doesn't stop Kirsty and her sayings. She had one ready for Morag's prediction of trouble too: 'Disasters always come in threes, my old granny used to say.'

Kirsty's old granny said a lot. A bit like Kirsty.

'Come on,' I said to Tina as Dad headed upstairs to his office to try to check out the authenticity of Vladimir's document. 'Let's cheer ourselves up. Let's go and see the animals.'

We crossed the back yard to Donk and Lily's pen. Donk gave us a 'hullo' nod of his shaggy head. Lily did the same. She thinks Donk is wonderful and copies everything he does. If he picked up his hooves and did a donkey disco dance, she'd do the same.

'More trouble, Donk,' I said, scratching his nose. 'Someone else wants to put us out of business now. Right out of the Crumbling Arms too. But don't you worry, we won't let them. You and Lily will be fine.'

Donk moved his head for me to scratch round his ears. He didn't seem in the least worried.

'Who else have you got staying just now?' asked Tina.

'Come and see,' I said, and led the way to the other sheds and outbuildings that house our paying guests. I opened the door of the nearest one. 'Meet Shampers.'

'Oh, he's lovely,' breathed Tina. 'What exactly is he?'

'A ferret,' I said, opening up his cage and taking him out. 'He's called Shampers because his coat is the colour of champagne. He's really cute and very tame.'

'So I see,' laughed Tina, as Shampers ran up my arm and curled himself round my neck like a furry scarf. 'He looks really soft and cuddly. Can I hold him?'

'Only if you don't mind the smell,' I grinned. 'He does pong a bit and it tends to linger . . .'

But Tina didn't mind. When she'd lived in London, she wasn't able to have any pets, but now she had Micky, a greyhound we had both rescued, and was just as mad on animals as I was.

'Where is Micky?' I asked, suddenly realising he wasn't with her.

'Watching Mum dye her wool. He's a very curious dog. Poked his nose into a tub of dye the other day and it came out blue. But Mum says it'll soon wear off. She's just had some good news; she's got a commission from a really posh shop in Edinburgh to make some scarves for them. They're going to take some of Dad's funny-shaped pots too. Said they were very fluid and organic or something.'

'Great,' I said. 'Their craft business might be starting to take off.'

We put Shampers back in his cage and I opened up the next one.

'Oh, you've got a Mrs Tiggywinkle,' smiled Tina. 'She's lovely, but not quite so cuddly.'

'She came in last night. She was lucky, she was just stunned by a passing car and will be fine in a few days.'

We get so many hedgehogs to look after. They're hopeless at crossing roads. I wanted to paint hedgehogs on the zebra crossing at the edge of Auchtertuie to alert motorists to them, but Constable Ross said that wasn't allowed, and anyway they wouldn't be seen very well in the dark. I didn't tell him I was going to use luminous paint.

'Can't you put up a sign that says "Hedgehogs Crossing"?' asked Tina. 'I've seen signs like that for frogs.'

'I thought of that, but Dad made me phone up the Highways department to see if it was all right.'

'And?'

'It wasn't. Would you believe I would have to get permission from the Scottish Parliament first, and by the time that happened, I could be an old lady and hedgehogs could be extinct. I could just do it anyway, I suppose, but then Constable Ross would know it was me, and Dad would be cross. He's so law-abiding, my dad. But don't worry, I haven't given up on the idea. I'll think of something . . .'

At that moment the door opened and Samantha slid in. She gave us an aristocratic stare then tiptoed daintily towards us. I stooped to stroke her, but she took one sniff, wrinkled up her pretty little Siamese nose and turned tail.

'She obviously doesn't like the smell of ferret,' grinned Tina.

'Not posh enough for her,' I said. 'Even if he is called Shampers.'

The door opened again as Millie and Max came looking for us too. Millie sat and gave Tina a polite paw. Max stuck his nose in her pocket just in case there was anything in there to eat.

'Stop scrounging, Max,' I said. 'Come along and I'll see if I can find you a dog biscuit.'

Max gave me a look that said, 'I'd much rather have a human-being biscuit, preferably covered in thick layers of chocolate, but, if a dog biscuit's really the best you can do . . .'

We wandered back to the kitchen. Kirsty was up

to her elbows in haddock and prawns, making preparations for her celebrated fish pie.

'Ah, there you are, Kat. Put the kettle on, would you? Constable Ross will be in soon for a cup of tea.'

'How do you know that?' I grinned. 'You've not been developing the power of the second sight as well? Morag won't be best pleased.'

'No.' Kirsty shook her head. 'He phoned a few moments ago to say he'd be over. He needs to talk to your dad. He's had a complaint from that Vladimir character. It seems he now wants your dad arrested.'

'Whaaaaat!!!!'

Vladimir could have heard my yell from the bowels of his tartan boat.

'I know,' said Kirsty. 'The man's obviously as nutty as a peanut patch. But Willie Ross will sort it out.'

I ran upstairs to find Dad. He was in his office – actually an old boxroom – going through the family papers which he kept in an ancient trunk.

'Dad!' I ran and hugged him. 'Have you heard? That that that . . . idiot has contacted Constable Ross and . . .'

'I know. I know, Kat. Calm down.'

'But why? What's happened? What . . . ?'

'He must have been really annoyed about losing his wig and people laughing at him. He phoned Willie Ross to tell him that I'm an imposter. That I have no right to the Crumbling Arms, and that he can prove it. Willie Ross has to look into it, that's all.'

'All! But you have documents too,' I said, looking at the pile scattered on the desk.

'Oh yes,' said Dad. 'It's just that I can't find one that actually proves I own the inn.'

'But of course you own the inn. You've always owned it. There's no doubt about that.'

'Not until now,' said Dad.

Help! I bet even Kirsty's old granny didn't have a gloomy enough saying for this.

Chapter 7

We heard the clump of Willie Ross's size twelve boots and went downstairs to meet him. He was in the kitchen with Kirsty and Tina. He was still wearing his policeman's hat which he always does when his business is official.

'You're not going to arrest my dad, are you, Constable Ross?' I demanded, standing in front of Dad with my arms out wide. 'He's done nothing wrong.'

Millie and Max, hearing my tone, came and stood beside Dad too.

'Arrest your dad,' smiled Constable Ross, 'and risk the wrath of Kat McCrumble and her collies? I'd need a whole division of policemen for that.

No, no, I've just come to tell your dad that Vladimir McCrumble has put in a complaint to the effect that your dad is living in what he claims is his property, and he wants him out as soon as possible.'

'But Vladimir's a nutcase,' I protested. 'That's as plain as the nose on your face. No offence.'

Constable Ross nodded. 'Aye, and I expect your dad can prove his ownership of the Crumbling Arms, and it'll all be over in a day or two.'

Dad shook his head. 'Trouble is, Willie, I can't. I've been through the family papers and I can only trace our lineage so far.'

'But possession is nine-tenths of the law, isn't it, Constable Ross, and my grandfather and great-grandfather and lots of other great-greats, I can't remember now how many Dad told me, lived here, so we're entitled? Amn't I right?'

'Pity you're going to be a vet and not a lawyer, Kat,' said Constable Ross. 'You're partly right, but if Vladimir's claim is better than your dad's and he can prove it in court . . .'

'I can't afford to go to court,' said Dad, sitting down at the kitchen table and running his fingers distractedly through his hair. 'I'll just have to keep searching through the family documents to try to find the missing one.'

'Aye, and we'll all give you a hand if we can,

Hector,' said Constable Ross, taking off his hat. 'The man's obviously a bit cracked. Now did someone say something about tea? I always think better with a mug in my hand.'

Kirsty poured the tea and went back to making her fish pie while Tina and I wandered outside.

The tartan boat was still there. Faint sounds of Scottish country dance music floated over the loch towards us.

'That man cannot be for real,' I said. 'But he makes me so angry. Did you see the look on Dad's face in there? There must be something I can do to help.'

'But what?' asked Tina.

'Don't know,' I said, looking along the shoreline to Auchtertuie's little harbour. Then, 'Wait a minute, Tina. Do you fancy going fishing?'

'Why, hasn't Kirsty got enough for her fish pie?'

'Don't think fish pie, think fish spy. We could go out with Lachy McCrumble in his fishing boat and take a closer look at the tartan tub. Lachy's getting ready to cast off. Look.'

'Will he wait for us?'

'He will if you go now and tell him we're coming. I'll catch up with you.'

'But where are you going?'

'To get our spies' binoculars. See you in a minute.'

I flew into the inn, told Dad where we were going, then slipped out again with the two pairs of binoculars we keep in the lounge for the guests. Millie and Max came too. I knew Lachy wouldn't mind the dogs. Neither would his wife, Netta. She hailed me as I climbed on board.

'Hullo, Kat. Hullo, Tina. I see you want to take a closer look at the tartan boat too. It'll be good to have some company. Nice day for a wee sail. Hullo, Millie. Max, take your nose out of my shopping bag. You'll get your share of the sandwiches later.'

With a judder from its old engine, and a great deal of blue smoke, Lachy's boat eased away from the little harbour. It wasn't the only one. My idea about having a closer look at the tartan boat was shared by just about everyone in Auchtertuie. Anyone who had a fishing boat, a dinghy, a jet-ski or a swimming proficiency certificate was off to have a look. It's not that we're nosey or anything, but . . . As for my idea of doing a quiet bit of spying – no chance. We chugged out to look at the *McCrumble* as did everyone else. I got out my binoculars to get a closer view. Vladimir was on deck in his full Highland regalia, waving royally to everyone. He was obviously enjoying the attention. I scowled. If there had been a rotten fish available I'd have thrown it at him.

'He's loving every minute of this,' I muttered to Tina. I scanned the boat, but could see nothing that looked particularly suspicious. Some crew members were sitting at a table in the stern, playing cards and laughing uproariously. Then some of them got up and did a little dance, but perhaps that was because they knew people were watching.

I put down my binoculars. 'Not one of my better ideas,' I said. 'This doesn't help a bit.'

'Och, never mind, Kat,' said Netta, patting me on the hand. 'Things will work out. There's no way you'll be leaving the Crumbling Arms.'

Was there anyone in Auchtertuie now who didn't know what Vladimir wanted?

Netta took out her sandwiches and passed them round. I was too anxious to eat much so Max got most of mine.

When we got back ashore, I thanked Lachy and Netta, and said goodbye to Tina.

'Home,' I said to Millie and Max. Then thought 'Home?' But for how much longer?

'There must be something I can do to help,' I said to the dogs. 'But what?'

Chapter 8

Meantime, there was another concern. When I got home, Kirsty was in the kitchen, busy with the food for the evening diners, and Dad was outside in the little shed we use as a treatment room. Donald was there too.

'Hi, Donald,' I said, putting worries about Vladimir aside for a moment, 'have you brought us a new patient?'

'I'm afraid so, Kat,' Donald frowned. 'But I don't really think we can save him. I found him lying in the woods on the estate. He's in a bad way.'

'I've sent for the vet,' said Dad, 'but I think it might be too late.'

I looked at the peregrine falcon lying on the

table. It was about forty centimetres long and had its brown wings folded back. Its eyes were closed, and there seemed to be hardly any movement from its chest.

I smoothed its soft feathers and whispered to it gently. Peregrines are magnificent birds. I think they resemble sleek jet fighters as they dive towards their prey, which they catch in mid-air in their powerful talons. They don't usually have to worry too much about predators themselves, but something had obviously got to this one.

'What do you think happened to him?' I said. 'He doesn't look very old.'

'He's not,' said Dad. 'That's what's so puzzling. We have to find out what's gone wrong.'

But, by the time Fred Goldsmith, the vet, came out from Fort William, it was too late. The young peregrine had died.

I lined an old cardboard box with soft feathery grasses and laid the bird inside.

Fred Goldsmith patted my shoulder as I handed him the box. 'I know how you feel, Kat,' he said, seeing my solemn face, 'but sometimes there's nothing you can do to help. You just have to accept that. I'll take the bird away now and give you a call when I find out what happened to him.'

I left the shed and wandered back across the

yard and into the kitchen. Kirsty took one look at me and gave me a hug.

'The bird . . . ?' she said.

I nodded. 'I'm all right. It's just . . .'

'I know,' said Kirsty. 'How about giving me a hand? That'll help take your mind off it. Give your hands a good scrub and take that crème brûlée to table four.'

I scrubbed up and headed for the dining room with the pudding. The dining room was full and there was a good buzz of chatter and laughter. Kirsty was an excellent cook and people came from miles around to sample her food. There was one man, dressed in a dark suit and sunglasses, sitting at table four. The sun had gone in and I hoped he would be able to see his pudding. He was very polite.

'Perhaps he's a food inspector,' I thought, and was equally polite. 'Enjoy your pudding,' I said. 'Would you like coffee to follow? We have several different kinds which we serve with some of Kirsty's delicious tablet.'

I hope you're impressed with my impeccable manners!

The mystery man ordered a double espresso. Then I was kept busy clearing away plates and chatting to people about our animals, and about what was going on in the village. Of course, everyone wanted to know all about the tartan boat, and soon there was a general discussion about the Russian who thought he was clan chief.

'But surely your dad's the clan chief,' said Eric, who was sitting at the window table with his two younger brothers.

'He is, I suppose, except . . .'

'He would never think to call himself that, would he?' said Thomas. 'In all the years we've been coming here, I've never even heard him refer to it.'

'No.' I shook my head. 'Dad always says it's the kind of person you are that's important, not the label that's attached to you.'

'Quite right too,' agreed the diners. 'He's a nice fellow, your dad.'

'Yes,' I agreed and cheered up a bit. I cheered up even more when nearly everyone slipped me a good tip as they left. Only the man in the dark suit and sunglasses left without saying a word or leaving a tip. Oh well, I still had almost enough saved up now for a new Abandon Hope CD. They were my very favourite band.

I played one of their CDs as I got ready for bed that night. As usual, Millie and Max had followed me upstairs. As usual, Millie settled herself neatly down on the rug beside my bed, and, as usual, Max took a running jump at the bed and got into it before I did.

'Get down, Max,' I said, and he gave a deep sigh followed by an injured look and jumped off. *I* knew he would be back up on the bed as soon as I was asleep. *He* knew he would be back up on the bed as soon as I was asleep, but we went through the nightly ritual anyway. I felt I had to *try* to train him.

I had just put my head down on my pillow, which smelled rather comfortingly of collie, when I remembered that I hadn't cleaned my teeth. I was really tired and thought for a brief moment of not bothering. Then I had a sudden vision of Ali McAlly, our local taxi-driver, and his gummy smile. I got up immediately. Half asleep, I wandered along the hallway to the bathroom, and spread some stripy minty stuff on my toothbrush. I scrubbed up and down and up and down till I was sure I had removed all the remnants of the tablet I had pinched earlier. Then I rinsed out and wiped my mouth on my pyjama sleeve. I put off the bathroom light and was just about to sleepwalk back to my bed when I shivered in a sudden draught. An open door downstairs? I didn't think so. A movement at the top of the stairs caught my eye.

Immediately wide awake, I stood perfectly still.

Slowly, the ghostly form of Old Hamish appeared at the top of the stairs. His kilt and plaid were torn and worn in places, and his long grey hair hung untidily about his face. I wasn't afraid. I knew Old Hamish meant me no harm. He hovered slowly over to me, his old black shoes not quite touching the floor, and, as he had so often done in the past, he laid a hand on my arm. I felt no weight, only a slight chill. He looked at me kindly and was gone. Who knows where? But I knew what that hand on my arm meant. I knew it was a warning. A warning to me to be careful.

Chapter 9

Tina came over next morning with Micky. Micky was a much livelier dog than he had been when we rescued him from Millar's pond, and he greeted everyone with a happy wag of his tail. I stroked his smooth, sleek head and had just started to tell Tina and Kirsty about seeing Old Hamish when Henry McCrumble came into the kitchen. Henry is Auchtertuie's very best organiser. He organises the Highland Games every year, he organises coach tours from Auchtertuie to the rest of Scotland every summer, and he organises litter collections round Auchtertuie every autumn, after the tourists have gone. He would organise Kirsty too, if she would let him, but Kirsty is Auchtertuie's second-best organiser, and will have none of it.

The McCrumble clan seem to be made up of two different types of people: those who are organised and those who aren't. Henry is organised. His sister, Jillie, isn't. She wears odd socks, and not always on her feet. Well, one cold day she couldn't find her gloves, so why not? Kirsty is organised. Morag isn't. She sometimes mixes up the post. No wonder there are no secrets in Auchtertuie. I'm organised – what do you mean, Ho Ho Ho? – and Dad, well you know he isn't.

Henry had leaflets in his hand. You seldom see Henry without leaflets or posters or stickers about something or other, and today's leaflets were about the Grand Jumble Sale.

'Hullo, ladies,' he beamed at us. 'Look what I've brought for you. Will you put these leaflets in the lounge for the visitors, Kat? And, if you take some of them too, Tina, that'll save me a trip out to your place. I'm sure your mum and dad won't mind displaying them in the shop. We want to get a really good crowd at the sale this year, the cottage hospital needs money for a scanner. I hope you've all been collecting your jumble.'

We nodded. 'Oh yes.'

Well, I knew Tina had, because she told me she had a box filled with old toys and games that she'd finished with, and her mum and dad had a box of some of their craft stuff that hadn't quite worked. Like Mr Morrison's pots that had got a bit chipped in the kiln, and Mrs Morrison's pale green scarves that had turned out the colour of sick. And I knew Kirsty had, because the box sat in the corner of the kitchen, and had old table covers and odd cups put into it at regular intervals. There was another box too that contained jars of home-made chutney and jam and bottles of fruit. Nearer the time she would make loads of tablet and put that into the box, and I would go to the Grand Jumble Sale and buy it and eat it.

I did have a box. It sat in the corner of my bedroom. I put things into it at regular intervals too. Then I took them out again in case I might need them. Kirsty gets cross with me.

'And when exactly are you going to need a pair of stripy socks that fitted you when you were five years old, Kat McCrumble?' she'd ask.

'Well, I might want to make two little sock puppets one day.'

'And one half of a pair of rollerblades?'

'The other one might turn up.'

'What about your pink fairy wand? Tell me about that.'

'Now, that might really come in handy. A girl

never knows when she might need a pink fairy wand to get herself out of trouble.'

But I knew I would have to put something into the box. I would make my special oatie biscuits, of course, for the produce table, and also some pancakes on the day, if I had time. But, it was a jumble sale, and I would just have to find some jumble. From somewhere.

The back door opened and Morag arrived with the post, with Millie and Max at her heels.

'Ah, Morag,' said Henry. 'I was hoping to catch you here. Will you deliver some of these leaflets for me on your round?'

'Och yes,' said Morag, and put them in her bag. 'But first of all, I have news.'

Everyone sat round the table and waited expectantly. In that respect, all McCrumbles are the same, we're all nosey. It was rubbing off on Tina too.

'What is it, Morag?' she asked eagerly.

Morag paused to take a sip of tea, and a bite of scone, to prolong the agony.

'I've just come from the big hotel,' she said. 'It's on my rounds,' she added, as though we didn't know.

'And?' Kirsty prompted.

'Well, you know we found out that C.P. Associates,

who own the hotel as well as the estate, is really only one man?'

'And he's called Callum McCrumble, yes yes.' Kirsty was getting impatient.

'Well . . . he's here.'

'Here?' I squeaked. 'In Auchtertuie? Then I'd like a word or six with him.'

'He's staying at the hotel. Has a suite there apparently. Does business from it from time to time.'

'You heard this from Sarah?' asked Henry.

Sarah was a waitress at the big hotel and was the second cousin of Henry McCrumble's wife, Lottie. Don't worry if you can't work it out. I get confused too.

Morag nodded. 'He's been here for a few days. Arrived by helicopter. Nobody really knew who he was until now. It seems he was visited in his suite by Ron Jackson, and one of the porters overheard Ron Jackson call him Mr McCrumble. Then he saw Callum McCrumble frown and motion Ron to be quiet.'

'Does Sarah know the whereabouts of the suite?' I asked, as innocently as I could. I knew roughly the layout of the hotel, but there were several suites.

Apparently I don't do innocent very well though.

'No, she does not,' said Morag, 'and if she did I

wouldn't tell you, Kat McCrumble. You'd most likely go storming in there to give him a piece of your mind, and get us all in trouble. Especially me. And your dad would be furious.'

Moi? Go storming in? I put on my innocent look again, but still no one was fooled.

It was a pity Sarah didn't know where the suite was. I'd just have to work out another way of getting to see Callum McCrumble, and telling him exactly what I thought of him.

Morag had no more news so Henry left to get on with his leafleting. Tina and Micky and I walked him to the front door. The tartan monstrosity was still out in the loch, floating gently in the calm waters.

'If that Vladimir wasn't out to cause trouble for your dad, I'd consider rowing out there with my leaflets and inviting him and his crew to the jumble sale,' said Henry, 'but there's no way.' Then he said cheerio and left.

'There's someone else on their way out there now,' pointed out Tina. 'Isn't that the big hotel's speedboat?'

'I wonder if Callum McCrumble's on it,' I said, and raced into the lounge to get the binoculars. I ran back outside, focused them, and had a look. There was only one man on the speedboat. It wasn't

Callum McCrumble, but it was one I certainly recognised.

'It's Ron Jackson,' I said. 'Now why's he going out there? Is he just being nosey too?'

But, as I watched, Ron Jackson took the speedboat right alongside the *McCrumble*, secured it, then climbed up the ladder on to the big boat.

'He's no tourist. He's up to something,' I muttered to Tina. 'And you can be sure it's nothing good.'

I shuddered as a small shiver ran down my spine. Old Hamish had been right to warn me. There was trouble afoot. As though we didn't have enough already.

Chapter 10

Auchtertuie looks as though it's one of those quiet places where nothing much ever happens. That if a dog crosses the road it's big news. But Auchtertuie's not really like that at all. Lots of things happen. And it wasn't a dog crossing the road that was big news, it was Jinty's hens.

I like hens. They're inoffensive, clucky things that provide me with a tasty egg for my breakfast. They're a comforting sort of bird, nodding away to themselves like they're always holding a quiet, internal conversation.

'Now, what am I going to do today? I think I'll start off with a bit of pecking, followed by . . . a bit of pecking, followed by . . . oh, another bit of pecking, I shouldn't wonder. Then, I might think about laying an egg, and to finish off, probably a final bit of pecking. Yes, that should just about do it. Busy day. Busy day.'

Actually, I think hens are pretty dim. In Auchtertuie, they peck away along the shoreline, at nothing anyone else would want to eat, and generally mind their own business.

BUT . . .

Today was different. After Tina had taken Micky home, I went out to the yard with Millie and Max to feed the animals. Kirsty had some spare carrots so Donk and Lily were in for a treat. Emily, the tarantula, who often boards with us, had arrived to stay for a couple of days. Her owners were having Granny come to stay, and Granny was an arachnophobe. I love that word, arachnophobe. It sounds like a sneeze. *A-A-A-RRRACHNO – PHOBE*. Bless you. Use your hanky, not your sleeve. But Emily wasn't scary. Hairy, but not scary. She was a big softy really, and liked to run up and down my arm for a bit of exercise. After I had fed Donk and Lily, I stopped at her vivarium for a chat. She seemed pleased to see me, though it's not easy to tell with a tarantula. They don't actually give you a big toothy grin like you see in the cartoons. Then I looked in on Shampers and Mrs Tiggywinkle.

Shampers was having a quiet snooze and the hedgehog was much better. She was up on her feet and snuffling about. We would be able to release her quite soon.

I headed back into the kitchen and found we had some other visitors. Sitting there snuggled down by the warm stove were four of Jinty's hens.

'Hullo, how did you get here?' I asked, which was a pretty stupid question. Our front door is always open and anyone is welcome to wander in. Millie went over and gave the hens a curious, but not unfriendly sniff. Max sat back on his hind legs and looked confused. Not that it takes a lot to confuse Max. He knew about Jinty's hens. He knew he saw them every day. He knew he wasn't allowed to chase them. He knew they didn't want to play ball with him. He knew they pecked along the lochside. What he didn't know was what they were doing in his kitchen. He gave me a questioning little *wuff*.

'I don't know what they're doing here either, Max,' I said. 'I'd better take them back across the road.'

I stooped to pick up the hens. 'But look what they've left us,' I said, and put the four brown eggs they'd been sitting on up on to the kitchen table. Then I put the hens into an old basket and carried them across the road to the lochside.

I wasn't the only one in Auchtertuie carrying hens that day.

Evie McCrumble from the post office was bringing hens back too, as was Luigi McCrumble from the chippie and Mario McCrumble from the hairdresser's.

'Don't know what's got into these hens today,' Mario muttered.

'Perhaps they wanted a haircut,' I grinned.

Mario looked at my unruly hair. 'No, but you could be doing with one, Kat. I never admit to people that you're one of my clients. It's bad for business.'

What a cheek. My hair wasn't too bad. If I tied it up in two scrunchies, I could still see out from under the fringe. Almost.

Mario and I chatted for a few minutes till I saw Kirsty come back with the shopping, then I went to tell her about the hens and the four brown eggs.

Kirsty laughed, 'Och well, eggs don't come any fresher than that. I can use them in the sponges I'm just about to make for the Lifeboat ladies' afternoon tea.'

The Lifeboat ladies come from all round the Auchtertuie area and meet in the lounge of the

Crumbling Arms on the third Thursday of every month. They always talk about their latest efforts to raise money for the Lifeboat charity to begin with, but, once that's done, the gossiping begins. Going out and in with their tea and cake, I could always find out who was having a baby, who had been on a fantastic holiday, and who was on a strict diet, although never on the third Thursday of the month because no one could resist Kirsty's cakes.

Today was no exception. Kirsty had made two wonderfully light sponges, sandwiched them with her home-made lemon curd, iced them and put little strands of lemon zest on the top. The ladies drooled when they saw them.

'What about the diet?' asked one.

'We'll start that tomorrow,' said her friend.

'Anyway, one little slice won't hurt,' said another. Then the ladies proceeded to demolish both cakes, leaving very few crumbs for the birds.

I kept them supplied with tea, but I don't think they noticed. They were too busy chatting. I went in to clear away the tea things, but I don't think they noticed that either. One of them, the president of the committee, I think, had started to sing an old Scottish song.

'Westering home and a song in the air
Light in the eye and it's goodbye to care . . .'

'I don't know what's got into them today,' I said to Kirsty as more of them joined in the singing.

'Laughter and love and a welcoming there
Isle of my heart my own one.'

'Perhaps they're giving a concert to raise funds for the lifeboat and are practising,' said Kirsty.

But the singing grew louder and louder followed by much giggling, followed by several ladies dancing up the hall past the kitchen door.

'What on earth . . . ?' said Kirsty.

We went to take a closer look. This wasn't like the Lifeboat ladies at all.

We passed the dancing ladies in the hall and came upon the dancing ladies in the lounge. They were doing a kind of eightsome reel, though their arithmetic wouldn't have pleased my maths teacher. They tried to get Kirsty and me to join in as they decided that the Crumbling Arms was too small and that they would be much better dancing in the street. They danced out of the front door and on to the road, causing traffic to swerve, drivers to mutter, and a small, interested crowd to gather.

The ladies didn't seem to care.

'Something's very wrong, Kat,' frowned Kirsty. 'We must get them back indoors.'

But they didn't want to come.

'Go away and don't be such spoilsports,' they giggled to Kirsty and me when we tried to persuade them.

'We have to do something, Kat,' said Kirsty. 'Before there's an accident. Tell you what, I'll go inside and lock the back door, while you get the ladies to join you in a conga. Then lead them back into the Crumbling Arms, and I'll nip round and lock the front door after them.'

Get the Lifeboat ladies to join me in a conga! She had to be joking!

But one look at her serious face told me she wasn't. Reluctantly I went up to the president, who was by this time careering up and down the street in her own version of 'Strip the Willow'. I took a deep breath.

'How about a conga,' I suggested, as quietly as I could.

'A conga!' she screeched. 'What a splendid idea, my dear.'

She had just ruined my street cred for ever. The Nisbet boys, who were in the crowd that had gathered, thought it was hilarious. They laughed and yelled, 'Cool, Kat. Really cool.' I'd never live it down.

I'd never done a conga before, and had only ever seen it done by daft people on the telly, but I knew it involved holding the waist of the person in front of you and kicking your legs in the air. So, I did my best. My trainers stayed on, but several pairs of expensive high heels flew off into the road, and were left there. But Kirsty's plan took shape, and with me at the head of the line, we conga'd up and down the street a couple of times. Then, when I hoped the ladies wouldn't notice, I led them singing and dancing back into the Crumbling Arms. Kirsty immediately locked the front door behind us. Now we had the whole of the Lifeboat ladies' committee locked in the Crumbling Arms. And you think a hairy tarantula is scary!

Actually the ladies were OK. After all their exertions, they were tired out, and fell into the chairs in the lounge and went to sleep. You could have heard their snoring in Inverness. Not even the loud banging of Constable Ross's fist on the front door wakened them.

I opened the door.

'I believe you have had a bit of an unusual incident here, Kat,' he said. 'Would you like to tell me about it?'

Dad arrived back from the cash and carry just as Kirsty and I were relating our tale.

'What's going on?' he wanted to know. 'I can't turn my back for two minutes, but you lot are up to something.'

Constable Ross listened to the story. 'And the ladies were perfectly all right when they arrived, you say?'

I nodded. 'They had their meeting, then started to gossip over their tea and cake as they always do. Shortly after that, the singing and dancing began. Now they're snoring their heads off.'

'Did they have anything to drink?' asked Constable Ross.

'Only their usual tea,' I said, and pointed to the canister. 'It's the same tea you always have.'

Constable Ross nodded. 'What about the cake?'

Kirsty sighed. 'It was a plain iced sponge, Willie. Filled with my lemon curd. You've eaten similar a million times.'

'What goes into a sponge?'

Kirsty sighed again. 'You'll be wanting baking lessons next. There was flour, sugar, margarine, eggs. Eggs fresh from Jinty's hens that laid them in here this morning.'

'What were the hens doing in here?'

Kirsty shook her head. 'Having a holiday. A change of scene. I don't know.'

'Kirsty doesn't speak hen,' I grinned. 'But you could always try Morag. She might be able to communicate.'

Constable Ross took off his hat and became Willie. 'I was having a haircut this morning when some of Jinty's hens wandered into Mario's. Now that's unusual too.'

So was his haircut. Mario must have been talking too much and not looking at what he was doing. Still, Willie Ross's hair would grow. Given time.

'Is there anything left of the cake?' he asked suddenly.

'A few crumbs,' I said, and pointed to the plates, still on the tray on the kitchen table.

Willie Ross produced a plastic evidence bag and carefully scooped the crumbs into it. 'I need to have these analysed,' he said.

'Are you saying my baking caused this?' Kirsty was annoyed. 'How often have you eaten my cakes, Willie Ross, and *you* haven't started dancing in the street!'

'It's not your baking, Kirsty,' he soothed. 'I just have to check the contents, that's all. Meantime, I'll go and get the police wagon and ferry these ladies home. There is no way they are in a fit state to drive.'

Help! The Lifeboat ladies being taken home in the police wagon. Whatever next?

Chapter 11

I lay in bed that night and had a worry. All the events of the last few days whizzed round and round in my brain. I was so busy worrying about them, I didn't even tell Max off for climbing up on to my bed. He lay on my feet, gently snoring.

Vladimir McCrumble and his claim to the Crumbling Arms was the first thing I worried about. He was a real problem. Dad still hadn't found anything among the family papers to actually prove, without doubt, that we were the real owners of the Crumbling Arms, that he was the real clan chief.

'What I need, Kat,' he'd said to me, 'is a will. A will from Old Hamish's father to say that the castle was left to Hamish, since he was the elder twin. But that was probably lost when the castle fell into ruin, and without it, looking at Vladimir's document, his claim might be just as good as ours. The lawyers would have to decide, and we don't have the money for that. Even if we had, and were successful, we would only have spent lots of money to be exactly where we are now, owners of the crumbling Crumbling Arms.'

'But if we don't,' I'd said, 'we'll have no home, and neither will the animals or the wildlife. Who will look after them when they're in trouble?'

'I don't know, Kat,' said Dad, and he'd run his fingers through his hair and tugged at it, the way he always does when he's really worried.

I was really worried too, but still didn't know how I could help. There must be something I could do. But what?

Another worry was why Ron Jackson was going out on the hotel speedboat to see Vladimir. He had to be up to something. Whenever Ron Jackson was involved in anything, there was always trouble. But, no matter how much I thought about it, I didn't come up with any answers, so I decided to worry about something else.

That poor young peregrine. He shouldn't have died. What had happened to him? Running a wildlife sanctuary, you get to know a bit about the habits of the wildlife. For example, I know to look out for the red squirrels and their mad, mating chases during January and February. Several males will chase a female for ages, spiralling up and down tree-trunks, making spectacular, death-defying leaps through the tree canopy. I often slip into the forest on the edge of the estate to search for them. If I can find a bit of cover and sit very, very still I can watch their antics undetected. Did you know that baby squirrels are called kittens, and are born without teeth or hair? Mind you, so was I, till my hair grew in much the same colour as the red squirrels. My front teeth aren't quite so long, fortunately, though I do have a passion for nuts, preferably covered in chocolate.

And I know, when I'm in the forest in springtime, to look out for the young deer. Their greatest protection against predators is their wonderful camouflage. They lie very still in the undergrowth, not moving a muscle when danger threatens. I nearly tripped over one once, so now I really look where I'm going. The last thing I'd want to do is harm the wildlife.

But something had harmed that young peregrine.

Then I put the peregrine worry aside. Nothing could be done about that till Fred Goldsmith, the vet, got back to us.

What else was there to worry about? Ah yes, the strange behaviour of Jinty's hens and the Lifeboat ladies. That was a mystery rather than a worry. Perhaps Constable Ross and his little bag of crumbs could solve that one.

That just left me with the appearance of Old Hamish and that warning hand on my arm. What did I have to watch out for? I made a mental list.

Vladimir? Certainly.

Ron Jackson? Always.

Something happening in the forest to the peregrines? Possibly.

The walkabout hens and the dancing ladies? Who knows?

All these things floated round and round in my head. Restlessly I turned over in bed and disturbed Max. He gave a louder snore in protest. Millie raised herself up from my bedside rug and laid her head on the edge of my bed. She knew I wasn't asleep. She knew there was something wrong. I stretched out a hand and stroked her silky ears.

'What's going to happen, Millie?' I said. 'What's going to happen to Dad and me and all the people who work at the Crumbling Arms? What's going to happen to all the animals? Who'll look after Donk and Lily? Who'll feed Flip his favourite cat food? Where will Emily go when Granny comes to stay?'

Millie snuffled softly and licked my hand. She didn't know either.

I turned over again and tried to get to sleep. 'Be sensible, Kat McCrumble,' I told myself sternly. 'Just put everything out of your mind, at least till the morning, or else you'll be tired and grumpy, and no help to anyone.' And I had nearly succeeded too, and was just dropping off to sleep, when I remembered something else. Callum McCrumble. Why was he living in Auchtertuie? Was he up to something? Did it involve us? Should I add him to my list? Was his arrival something else I had to worry about?

I gave a deep sigh. It was all getting to be too much, even for me.

Chapter 12

Next day the Crumbling Arms fell down.

OK, not all of it. I'm being a little dramatic, I suppose. But some of it fell down. The lounge chimney fell down. Bits of it.

The day started off as usual with breakfast for the overnight guests. We had a lovely Japanese couple staying with us who spoke about the same amount of English as I do Japanese. I can say 'Sayonara', but saying goodbye is not much good when you're trying to ask people what they'd like for breakfast. They sat at the table in the window to admire the view over the loch, and I handed them a menu. They looked at it blankly. I turned it the right way up for them. That didn't help. I pointed at the tea and toast Dad was bringing in for some of the other guests. They nodded enthusiastically. That was fine.

'I'll bring you some in a moment,' smiled Dad, and left me to it. His Japanese was as good as mine.

So I tried pointing at the menu and miming some of the choices. I oinked like a pig for the bacon and the sausages. They obviously thought this was an old Scottish custom and tentatively oinked back. I smiled. This was getting tricky. I looked at the menu. How on earth could I mime porridge or black pudding? I refused to even consider waggling my rear end and clucking like a hen laying an egg.

Then Martin Murray, the fishmonger, came to my rescue. He drew up outside the Crumbling Arms in his fish van.

'One moment.' I held up my right index finger to the Japanese folks, and flew outside. Martin was just opening the back doors of his van to begin unloading.

'Emergency, Martin!' I cried. 'Have you any kippers today?'

'Certainly have.' Martin pointed to a gleaming, refrigerated display. 'How many do you want?'

'Dad will know how many we need,' I said, 'but can I just borrow two pairs for a moment?'

Martin sighed. 'Only you, Kat McCrumble, could ask to borrow kippers.' But he waved his consent and I grabbed some polythene wrappers and carried two pairs of kippers into the dining room.

The Japanese couple had been watching me and were ready with their answer as soon as I showed them the kippers. They smiled broadly and nodded that they would have them for breakfast. Great. I could forget donning my snorkel and goggles and wiggling like a fish.

BUT. Memo to self and Dad. Scan photographs of food on to menu cards. Even if the other guests did enjoy my antics . . .

Breakfast was almost over and the guests were just lingering over coffee when we heard a rumble.

'Thunder?' asked one.

I frowned. I looked out of the window. I could see the top of the Ben, which meant it wasn't raining. And the sky was clear. Anyway, the noise had sounded closer to home. I checked that the guests had everything they needed and slipped out into the hall. Dad was nowhere around. Probably gone outside to feed the animals. Unless he was tidying up in the lounge. I opened the door to look in and was met by a cloud of dust.

'What on earth . . . ?' I coughed, and stepped into

the lounge, quickly closing the door behind me to prevent the dust escaping out into the hall. Then I went to investigate. Despite the thick dust, it didn't take too long to discover the root of the problem. Some of the stones from the old fireplace were lying in the hearth, while others had tumbled out on to the elderly, faded rug.

'Oh no, how did that happen?' I muttered. 'And it's yet another problem. Poor Dad.' I hated to have to tell him, but I had no choice. I hurried out into the back yard. As I suspected, Dad was attending to the animals.

'There's been a little problem with the fireplace in the lounge,' I said, as gently as I could.

Dad immediately stopped mucking out Donk and Lily's pen and came indoors to have a look.

'Not such a little problem, Kat,' he groaned, going down on his hands and knees and looking up the chimney. 'I don't know if Donald and I can fix this. It may need a proper stonemason. There may be other stones loose inside the chimney. We can't take the risk of them falling and injuring someone. I'll phone Johnnie McAllister right away, and get him to come as soon as he can, but he's always so busy.'

Johnnie McAllister is Ali McAlly's younger brother, but you would never have guessed. There is absolutely no resemblance. Johnnie has all his own teeth and hair for a start, and is well known in the entire area for his wonderful way with stone. He can fashion it into anything at all, and his dry stane dykes are works of art.

'You make sure the guests are all right, Kat,' Dad went on, 'and I'll clear up this mess. Fortunately we don't need the fire in this good weather. That's always something.'

Dad was determined to be positive so I did my best too. I put on my smiley face as I waved goodbye and sayonara to our guests as they set out on their day. Then I started clearing the breakfast dishes into the kitchen. Kirsty arrived and gave me a hand. I had just finished telling her about the fireplace when Morag appeared with the post. She had on her solemn face.

'Where's your dad, Kat?'

'In the lounge, clearing up,' I replied, and told her about the fallen stones. 'We've to stay out till Dad hoovers up or the dust will get everywhere, he says.'

Morag nodded and sat quietly with her cup of tea and her scone. She had only taken a few sips when Dad came into the kitchen, his hands and face covered in grey dust. His hair was grey too and made him look older and more worried than ever.

But he smiled. 'Anything in the post, Morag?'

Morag gave a sad little sigh and handed him an official-looking letter.

'I'm afraid it's not good news, Hector,' she said.

Chapter 13

Dad opened the letter and read it. 'You're right, Morag,' he said. 'It's not good news. It's from Vladimir's lawyers, informing me of his intention to challenge my right to the title of clan chief of the McCrumbles and to the ownership of the Crumbling Arms. It's official now. I suppose I had been hoping a miracle would happen, and it wouldn't come to this.'

Morag pushed Dad gently into a chair, and Kirsty handed him a cup of tea.

'What are you going to do, Hector?' asked Morag. 'Whatever it is, we're behind you, and so are the rest of the McCrumbles in Auchtertuie. The cheek of yon Vladimir thinking he could just swan into

Auchtertuie and declare himself clan chief of the McCrumbles.'

'Aye,' said Kirsty, hands on hips. 'Just let him try setting one foot in my kitchen, and he'll find out where the shoe grips him. Clan chief indeed. Just who does he think he is?'

I gave Dad a fierce hug, spilling some of his tea on to his dusty lap, though he didn't notice. But there was something else bothering me. Something niggling away at the back of my mind. Something I couldn't quite reach . . . but before I could think about it any more, the phone rang.

I went to answer it. It was Fred Goldsmith.

'Hi, Kat,' he said. 'I've just had the test results back on that young peregrine that died the other day. I'm afraid he was poisoned.'

'Poisoned!'

'Yes. From the results it looks like he'd been pecking at his prey, a pigeon, I reckon, which had been laced with poison.'

'You mean it was deliberate? Someone put out a poisoned pigeon intending to kill the peregrines?'

'Looks that way,' said Fred. 'Some folks reckon the peregrines kill game birds, and so they try to kill them instead. It's illegal, of course, but that doesn't stop them.'

'But who . . . ?' I asked, though I already had a very good idea.

'Don't know,' said Fred, 'and it'll be very difficult to prove. That's the problem. Just keep an eye out. Perhaps Donald might see something in his travels through the estate.'

'I'll tell him. Thank you,' I said as I rang off.

Dad and Morag and Kirsty looked at me. They had gleaned enough from my side of the conversation to know what had happened.

'Ron Jackson's to blame,' I said. 'He's always on about the wildlife taking the game that he raises for the hotel guests to shoot. Anyway, who else would do such a thing?'

Dad nodded. 'But proving it will be a different matter, Kat. Ron Jackson's shown himself to be a slippery customer in the past. Always managed to cover his tracks. And you just can't go accusing people with no evidence.'

'I know,' I frowned. Constable Ross had said that to me often enough in the past.

'We'll all just have to keep a lookout,' said Morag, standing up to leave. 'I'll alert everyone on my rounds. Tell them to phone you or Willie Ross if they notice anything suspicious.'

Kirsty said nothing, just started banging pots and pans around, a sure sign that she was agitated. It was probably a bit early for her to start on the malt whisky she kept in the jar marked, 'Flour'. She only resorted to that when she was really upset.

It was time to leave the kitchen. Dad went upstairs to get cleaned up, and I phoned Tina to say I'd be along to see her. Perhaps talking things over with her would help.

I called Millie and Max to heel. Millie came. Max thought 'heel' meant dance about in front of me like an idiot and trip me up. I pushed him gently round to my side to remind him. He gave me his, 'Oh, so that's what you want me to do,' look. 'Why didn't you say so?' He was definitely a slow learner, that dog.

We left the Crumbling Arms and walked along the shore road towards Tina's. It was a slow journey. Everyone now knew about our problem with Vladimir and they stopped to chat.

'How's your dad, Kat?' asked Evie McCrumble, coming out of the post office with a sweetie for Millie and Max. 'Tell him I was asking kindly for him.'

I thanked her and wandered on.

Henry McCrumble came out of the chippie as I walked past.

'Ah, Kat,' he said, and lowered his voice to a whisper. 'I've just been to see Luigi and Mario and Lachy, and all the men from the tug-of-war team. Tell your dad, if he needs any help with any interlopers,' and he nodded at the tartan boat still out on the loch, 'we're ready and waiting.'

'Thank you,' I said. Henry, the organiser, had already been busy, but what Constable Ross would have to say about the McCrumble warriors taking on Vladimir's sailors, would be another matter.

When I eventually got to Tina's, she was outside in their little front garden, grooming Micky. He was loving it. His eyes were half closed in contentment as Tina stroked the soft brush over his lean frame. Then he and Millie and Max went off to play their 'who can find the most disgusting smell' game. Micky was happy with the other dogs now that he had learnt how to play. That was something he'd never experienced being reared as a racing dog.

Tina saw my troubled face and put an arm round my shoulders. 'Has something else happened, Kat?' she asked.

I nodded and told her about the letter and the peregrine.

'Ron Jackson's to blame for the peregrine,' she said immediately.

'I know,' I said. 'He and his boss, Callum McCrumble, are at the bottom of all the problems we have around here.'

Then a thought struck me. The one that had been hovering on the edge of my mind. I started to make connections. Callum McCrumble. Ron Jackson. The tartan boat. I'd seen Ron Jackson go out there. Could Callum McCrumble have sent him? Could Ron Jackson and Callum McCrumble be at the root of Dad's problems *this* time too? Callum McCrumble had tried often enough before to get hold of the Crumbling Arms. Could he be behind this latest attempt?

I talked it over with Tina.

'It's possible, Kat,' she said.

I nodded. 'But what can I do about it? If I tell Dad, he'll say it's a bit far-fetched and tell me to keep out of trouble. If I tell Constable Ross my suspicions, he'll say the same.'

'So what can you do, Kat?' said Tina. 'You're just a girl. You can't take on lawyers and millionaires and horrible gamekeepers all at once.'

Oh couldn't I indeed? I'd soon see about that.

Chapter 14

Tina decided to come back with me to the Crumbling Arms for lunch. She often does that. Her mum's not a very good cook. That day there was something liquid with an unidentifiable smell slurping around in a large pot on top of the hob. Cautiously, Tina lifted the lid and we looked in.

'What do you think it could be?' Tina asked.

I shook my head. 'Could be anything. Wallpaper paste, molten glue, a new cure for footrot? Who knows? Are you sure it's for lunch? Perhaps it's a dye your mum's cooking up to colour her wool or something.'

We looked in again. The mixture heaved and

glugged. Foamy, grey scum rose to the surface, floated to the edges, then clung to the side of the pot in a horrible, yucky ring.

'Whatever it is, I don't fancy it,' said Tina.

'Why don't you come home with me for lunch then?' I grinned.

'I thought you'd never ask,' Tina grinned back.

We went to tell Tina's mum where we were going. She was in one of the little sheds at the back of their house, sitting at her old spinning-wheel, busily spinning the sheep's wool she collects from the wire fences round about. Her grey-black hair hung down her back, caught up with what looked very much like pleated, hairy, blue string. She saw me looking at it.

'Hullo, Kat,' she smiled. 'What do you think of my latest idea? Evie McCrumble, at the post office, often has odd bits of hairy string left over from parcels, and I thought I might be able to recycle it. I've dyed this bit with woad and I'm just testing how well it keeps my hair in place. I might ask David to make me a few clay beads that I could add to the ends, so that it would jangle when I move my head. What do you think?'

I thought she was barking.

'What an interesting idea,' I said. You didn't know I was a diplomat, did you?

'I could make one for you, if you like. I'll dye the string green, though, that would be better with your hair colouring, and some nice terracotta beads would just finish it off.'

Oh help, that was all I needed to complete my scruffy look; my hair tied up with hairy green string and clay balls. Kirsty would go ballistic.

'Thank you, that would be lovely,' I managed to say. Well, you can't be rude to your best friend's mum, can you?

'I'm going to have lunch at Kat's, Mum,' said Tina, rescuing me before I found myself agreeing to wear anything even more outlandish.

'Oh, but what about my new recipe? What about the nettle and mixed herb soup?'

So that's what it was.

'Billy will eat it,' said Tina. 'He said he was working in the area today and would nip home for some lunch.'

Billy is Tina's big brother. He's an electrician with very little sense of taste or smell. He's also a Trekkie and gets dressed up in Trekkie outfits to go to conventions all over the country. Need I say more?

We escaped with Millie and Max. Micky stayed with Tina's mum. He curled himself up at her feet and closed his eyes. He was turning out to be one lazy dog. Fortunately he didn't have to worry too much about lunch; his came out of a tin.

Kirsty makes all our food from scratch from fresh ingredients, so there are very few tins at the Crumbling Arms. There's Samantha's tinned cat food, of course, which she reluctantly shares with Flip the badger. He seems to know the minute the food's been put in Samantha's dish, for his black snout comes through the cat flap, closely followed by the rest of him, then he pads over to the dish and scoffs the lot. There probably aren't many people who have to buy extra tins of cat food to feed the local badger.

There were no badgers in the inn at lunch-time, but Kirsty was feeding plenty of people. Lunch for the tourists was always a simple affair of soup and filled rolls, served in the bar. And the bar was noisy and crowded. Tina and I headed into the kitchen to help ourselves. Millie came with us. Max sneaked into the bar to see if he could scrounge a bit of anyone's roll. He had such an appealing face and pleading eyes that he usually succeeded. The soup of the day was smoky bacon and tomato, one of our favourites, so Tina and I got ourselves some bowls and spoons and tucked in. Kirsty looked sympathetically at Tina. She knew about Mrs Morrison's cooking skills.

'What was your mum making for lunch today?' she asked.

'She said it was nettle and mixed herb soup,' said Tina, 'but it looked more like . . .'

'Smelly gloop,' I finished for her.

'Och well, she can't be good at everything,' said Kirsty, 'and she's a really nice lady. I bought one of her scarves last week to send to my friend in Southend. She likes unusual things.'

We were just finishing off our soup when Dad brought through some plates from the bar.

'That's the last of the customers attended to,' he said. 'What a busy lunch-time.'

But it wasn't over yet. The kitchen door opened again and Constable Ross appeared.

'Would that be smoky bacon and tomato soup I can smell, Kirsty?' he asked.

'It would,' said Kirsty.

'And would there be a drop left over for a hungry policeman?'

'There might be if Kat and Tina haven't scoffed the lot,' said Kirsty, looking in the big pot and ladling out the last of the soup.

Constable Ross sat down at the table, took off his hat and became Willie Ross.

'I'm glad you came by, Willie,' said Dad. 'I was going to phone you. We had the test results on that young peregrine this morning. He was poisoned.'

'I know,' Willie muttered, through a mouthful of crusty bread. 'Fred Goldsmith phoned to tell me. It's a real problem, and very hard to find the culprits. The wildlife detectives do their best, but they have thousands of acres to patrol and they can't possibly be everywhere. We'll all just have to keep our eyes and ears open.'

'That's just what I thought,' I said.

Tina raised her eyebrows and gave me a look that said, 'Are you going to say anything about Ron Jackson?'

I gave her a look that said, 'Not at the moment.'

Willie Ross finished his soup and stood up.

'That was just grand, Kirsty. Thank you.'

Then he put his hat back on. 'I expect there will be people around here who will have their suspicions about who might be responsible for the poisoning of the peregrine,' he said. 'But I would have to remind those people that no one should be accused of anything without definite proof, and also that it is an offence to take the law into their own hands.' And, would you believe it, he looked directly at me.

I put on my totally innocent look. 'Moi?' it said. Moi?

But I could tell the look fooled nobody. Especially not Willie Ross with his policeman's hat on.

Chapter 15

After lunch Tina and I helped Kirsty fill the strawberry tart cases she had baked in the morning. We piled in the clotted cream, the strawberries and the strawberry syrup. The tarts *looked* delicious, but we had to taste them, just to make sure.

'It's quality control,' I told Kirsty, when she caught Tina and me on our third one. We just love strawberry tarts.

Kirsty's strawberry afternoon teas are legendary. People come from miles around to enjoy them. When we had finished making (and eating!) the tarts, Kirsty sent us into the lounge with trays of the pretty china she knew would be needed that afternoon. Dad had made a good job of cleaning up the lounge. There wasn't a speck of dust in sight. He had also tidied up all the fallen stones, and put an old firescreen, with a picture of Robert Burns, across the fireplace, so that the damage was hidden from view. And I knew he had phoned Johnnie McAllister to come as soon as possible to repair the chimney.

I had just set down my tray of crockery on the big oak sideboard when Tina nudged me and said, 'Kat, look!'

I looked. Through the lounge window I could see a rowing-boat approaching the shore. The boat held two men. One had bulging biceps and was pulling strongly on the oars, the other wore full Highland regalia. Vladimir. 'I want a word with him,' I said and ran outside.

'Kat, wait for me,' cried Tina.

I crossed the road and ran down the little beach. I reached the water's edge just as the boat scrunched ashore.

'What do you want this time? Haven't you caused enough trouble already?' I yelled at Vladimir. You'll notice that I didn't mince my words, that my diplomatic skills had completely deserted me.

Vladimir stepped out of the boat and smiled at me. He doffed his velvet tammie. His hair remained in place this time. He must have glued it on.

'Ah, you must be Kat, I think. Kat by name and cat by nature. Very scratchy and a little mad, I hear.'

'I am mad,' I yelled. 'Mad at you for all the trouble you've caused. So why don't you just go and sail your silly tartan boat elsewhere. You're not wanted here.'

But Vladimir's smile just widened, which annoyed me even more.

'But there is something I want,' he said. 'Something else I hear about is the strawberry cream teas at the Crumbling Arms. So, I come to try. Perhaps see if I might want to keep the . . . tradition, when the Crumbling Arms is mine. I am very fond of strawberries. Very fond of strawberry cream teas. This is good, no?'

And he walked past me, across the road, and headed for the inn. Tina and I ran after him. Dad was standing at the front door.

'Don't let him in, Dad,' I cried. 'He wants afternoon tea.'

'You serve afternoon tea to travellers?' Vladimir said to Dad.

'Yes.'

'Then I am traveller. I hear so much about Highland hospitality. I want afternoon tea . . . please,' he added, as an afterthought.

Dad stood aside to let him pass and Vladimir headed into the lounge.

I was apoplectic. Pacing up and down. Throwing my hands in the air. I couldn't believe it.

'Dad,' I yelled. 'What are you doing?'

'This is an inn, Kat,' said Dad. 'We serve the public. So long as Vladimir causes no trouble we are obliged to serve him too.'

'You must be joking,' I said. But I could see that he wasn't. My dad is just too . . . nice. He's from the Planet Polite. He's from the Galaxy of Good Manners. He's from the quiet, calm bit of the family. Guess who doesn't take after him at all?

'Well, I'm not serving him and neither is Tina,' I declared. Then I had second thoughts. If I served Vladimir I might be able find out something useful. Something that might help us. 'Oh all right, then. I will serve him,' I said.

Dad and Tina both looked confused at my sudden change of mind as I left them and marched into the lounge. By now Vladimir was examining the old paintings on the walls. The paintings showed forbidding skies, misty glens and shaggy Highland cattle with soulful eyes and enormous horns. The paintings all hung slightly askew. Or it may be that the paintings were straight and it was the walls that were the problem.

Vladimir turned round to look at me. 'Why all these cows are standing in water?' he asked. 'Is it because it rain so much in Scotland?'

'No,' I said, 'the artist couldn't draw hooves.'

Vladimir thought I was kidding. 'Ah, yes, good joke. Scottish joke. When I am chieftain I will learn Scottish jokes. I am very funny man.'

He could say that again. Just not funny ha ha. I swallowed my temper, refrained from kicking him on his tartan shins, and put on my sweetest voice.

'Afternoon tea will be served shortly,' I said, setting out a tea plate, cup and saucer on the coffee table. 'Do have a seat.'

'Yes, yes,' beamed Vladimir. 'You go get the strawberries, little girly. I shall make myself at home.'

Little girly! I was tempted to throw the crockery at him, but Tina arrived with a plate of strawberry tarts in the nick of time.

'Donald's called your dad out to the sanctuary,' she whispered. 'But your dad says, remember to stay cool, Kat, or you'll only make things worse. He says not to do anything silly.'

Do anything silly? Me? As if!

But I knew Dad was right. So I stayed cool. So cool I was icy.

Vladimir had seated himself in the old, deep

armchair with the dodgy springs. I hoped they would poke through and nip his bum. I handed him a floral napkin which he put on top of his sporran.

'You put your sporran to the side when you sit down,' I said. 'Don't you know anything?'

'Ah,' he said. 'I will learn these customs when I am here longer time. You can teach me if you like. You are crazy girl, I hear, but clever.'

'Clever enough to know you're a fraud,' I said. 'But why do you want to be here? Why do you want to put us out of our business and out of our home? You can't prove you're the clan chief. Your documents don't actually say that.'

Vladimir took a bite of his strawberry tart, looked at me and smiled. 'Neither do yours,' he said, 'or you would have told me. But the lawyers will sort it out. I can wait. Now bring me some more tea, these tarts are delicious.'

Before I could reply, Tina hurried in.

'Your dad needs you in the sanctuary, Kat, right away.'

I left Tina keeping an eye on Vladimir, who was still munching, and hurried out to the back yard. Dad and Donald were in the little shed we use as a treatment room. On the table were what looked like a family of peregrines. The two adults were in a bad way, eyes closed, barely breathing. The little one just looked bewildered.

'Oh no,' I said. 'Not more poisonings?'

'Looks like it, Kat,' said Donald. 'I found them on the estate. I was just heading to have a look at some of the trees near the foot of the Ben, when I came across them lying on the ground. The young one's OK, probably just hungry and anxious.'

Dad shook his head. 'Donald and I will do what we can for the older birds, but you take the little one, Kat, and settle him in a cage. Give him something to eat and drink and keep an eye on him.'

'OK,' I said, and thought how typical it was of Dad to forget all about his own problems and concentrate on the wildlife when they were in trouble.

I looked after the young peregrine as best I could and was just chatting to him reassuringly when Tina came to look for me.

'What's happening?' she asked, and I told her the story.

'Dad will phone the vet again, but it looks like the same as last time.'

'Poor birds,' said Tina. 'They're only trying to survive.'

I nodded grimly. 'We need to find out who's

doing this. We need to catch them at it.' Then I remembered about Vladimir. 'What about the tartan terror?' I asked. 'Has he gone yet?'

'Sneaked off without paying,' said Tina.

Now why didn't that surprise me? But my head was too full of other things to care.

Chapter 16

As we feared, the two older birds died, and Fred Goldsmith took them away for post-mortem.

'Keep an eye on the young peregrine, Kat,' said Dad. 'Just in case.'

But I thought he would be all right. He had perked up and was now eating everything I gave him and looking for more. Usually, when a bird or animal is fully recovered, we release them straight back into the wild, but I was reluctant to do this with the young peregrine. What if he went back and ate something that was poisoned? He'd been lucky once; he might not be so lucky a second time. It was a real dilemma. Wild animals and birds should be in the wild, it's where they belong. But . . .

I talked it over with Dad and Donald.

'The longer we keep him, the more tame he'll become, Kat,' said Dad.

'And he may become unable to fend for himself in the wild,' said Donald.

'I know that,' I said, 'but I could be sending him straight back out there to be poisoned.'

Dad and Donald nodded. There was no easy answer.

Finally it was Constable Ross who came up with a solution. Kind of.

Dad had phoned him to report the wildlife crime and he came over as soon as he could. I introduced him to Perry – that's what I decided to call the peregrine, predictable, I know – and I told Constable Ross about my dilemma.

'I see the problem, Kat,' he said, 'but there's one thing you haven't taken into account.'

'What's that?'

'Your instinct. Part of a policeman's job is learning to trust his instinct. Sometimes that's all we have to go on.'

'Oh. Right. OK.' But how did that help?

'So, what's your instinct telling you to do with Perry right now?'

'Keep him,' I replied immediately.

'Problem solved,' said Constable Ross. 'Keep him

safe till we get to the bottom of this business, then release him and see how he gets on. If he can't manage on his own, you'll just have another wild creature to look after. If he can manage, he can look after himself.'

I gave Constable Ross a hug. I don't know if you're actually supposed to do that to your local policeman, but he seemed quite happy about it, and he had taken a weight off my mind. Everything in my head had been going round and round in a real jumble.

Jumble! The Grand Jumble Sale to raise money for the scanner for the cottage hospital! I'd forgotten all about it.

I left Constable Ross to talk to Dad and Donald and headed indoors. Perhaps that was another problem I could solve. Now that I knew what I was doing with Perry, I would fill that box in my bedroom right now. There's nothing like a good clear-out to make you feel better, Kirsty's always saying to me. Well I needed to feel better after all that had happened so . . . to work.

I started in my wardrobe first. It's an enormous, old, dark-brown thing that I used to hide inside when I was little. It smells faintly of mothballs because Kirsty's always trying to stop the local moths from eating everything in sight. I know they eat little holes in my sweaters, but there are usually so many other holes where I've got caught up in barbed wire, or on the branches of a tree, or that Donk has chewed, that it doesn't much matter. But I decided to be ruthless. Anything that I hadn't worn in a while, or was too short, or not in fashion (that was a joke), or that Kirsty had bought me and I hadn't liked and had put to the back of the wardrobe, I put into the cardboard box for the jumble sale. Then I started on my chest of drawers. It had once matched the wardrobe, but was now faded by the sun to a pale honey-brown. I had just opened the top drawer when my bedroom door flew open and Max bounded in, followed, at a more sedate pace, by Millie.

'Hullo, you two. Have you come to help me have a good clear-out?'

Millie immediately sat at my feet to keep me company. Max immediately dived into the big cardboard box and came up wearing the woolly hat with the santas on it that I'd worn when I was little, i.e. last winter. I really would have to do something about my image.

'Get out of there, Max, unless you want to be sold as jumble.'

Max came out, decided there were better smells under my bed and dived under there. If he found a smelly sock that would keep him happy for ages.

Meanwhile, Millie was happy to give me her opinion on the things I held up for her inspection.

'What about this green and pink top?' I asked her.

She wasn't impressed. It went in the box.

'Matching cardi?'

That went in the box too. I'm just not a matching cardi sort of person. Millie obviously knew that.

Millie didn't like the glittery T-shirt with half of the glitter missing either, or the eye-watering, gorse-yellow shorts Morag had once bought for me in a sale. They went into the box too. Millie nodded her approval. This dog had taste. Before long the box was pleasingly full, and Kirsty was right about having a good clear-out, it did make me feel better. Max came out from under my bed, half-chewed sock in mouth, just as I was unearthing my fairy wand. I was just showing the two dogs its finer points – it certainly wasn't going in the box – when I heard Kirsty calling me.

'Kat, get changed and come and lend a hand in the dining room. Your dad's overbooked again and we're full to overflowing.'

'OK,' I yelled back, and went to the wardrobe. It was empty. I tried the chest of drawers. It was empty too.

'Oh dear,' I said, 'the clear-out didn't last long.' And I did a Max-like dive into the box and came out wearing the green and pink stripy top.

But I'm still not a matching cardi kind of person.

Chapter 17

It happened again. Jinty's hens went walkabout. Not into people's houses or shops this time, not into the Crumbling Arms, but out on to the road. Now, sometimes the odd idiotic one decides to play in the traffic, but never the entire flock before. One moment they were pecking away quite happily along the shoreline, the next they were having a hen disco in the middle of the road. They were flapping around, doing a sort of hiccuping cluck, legs going every which way. They seemed not to have a worry in the world. Hens are usually quite timid creatures, but on this occasion no amount of annoyed motorists furiously honking their car horns made any difference. The hens were oblivious. They just didn't care.

It was the noise of the horns that sent me scurrying outside to find out what was going on. Me and everybody else. Kirsty dusted the flour off her hands on to her apron and came too. So did Donald and Dad, closely followed by Millie and Max. Even Samantha slid round the corner of the Crumbling Arms to have a look. No one wanted to miss out on what was happening.

What was happening was that the road was entirely blocked by these delinquent hens. Jinty was out from the bakery, of course, trying to apologise to the motorists and shoo the hens back on to the loch shore at the same time. No chance. They wouldn't be shooed. Jinty started lifting them up one by one. Eggs rolled gently from underneath some of them. Jinty picked them up and put them in her overall pocket. I ran to give her a hand. So did Donald and Dad and Kirsty. There are only so many hens and eggs one person can carry at a time.

We soon had the road clear and the motorists and the watching tourists gave a cheer and went on their way.

'I just don't know what's got into these hens,' worried Jinty. 'That's the second time this week they've acted strangely. I think I'll need to keep them locked up. But it's such a shame, they're used to pecking along here, and have never been any bother till recently.'

She had hardly finished speaking when Constable Ross appeared on the scene.

'More trouble with the hens, Jinty?' he said.

'Aye. I just don't understand it, Willie. I don't know what's going on. There wasn't a full moon last night, was there? I've heard it said that some creatures can go a bit crazy when the moon's full.'

'There was no full moon, Jinty,' said Donald. 'I was out after dark and would have noticed.'

'Of course,' said Jinty. Everyone in Auchtertuie knew that Donald was an expert on that kind of thing.

'Oh well,' she went on, 'now that the traffic's cleared, maybe you'll all give me a hand to get them into their shed at the back of the bakery.'

Constable Ross nodded. 'Fortunately there's been no harm done this time, Jinty, but the hens could have caused an accident. Best keep them locked up for a while till I find out what's going on. Are they still laying as normal?'

Jinty indicated her bulging overall pocket.

'Do you mind if I take a couple of these?'

'Help yourself,' said Jinty. 'Take as many as you

like. Do you want them for your tea?'

'A poached egg's lovely on top of a bit of smoked haddock,' said Kirsty.

But Constable Ross shook his head. 'I don't want to eat the eggs. I want to send them away for analysis.'

'Just like you did with Kirsty's cake crumbs,' I said.

'Those results were inconclusive, the Lifeboat ladies didn't leave enough crumbs, but a whole egg might show us something.' And he went off, carefully clutching two brown speckled ones. We helped Jinty ferry the hens across the road to their shed at the back of the bakery and locked them in.

'Och, poor things!' said Jinty. 'I hate locking them away.'

But, at that moment, the hens didn't seem to mind. They were quite dozy and were already half asleep.

'Oh I do hope I don't have to have them P U T D O W N.' Jinty spelt it out. 'It's so unfair. They're usually no trouble at all.'

'Don't worry, Jinty,' said Dad. 'We won't let that happen. Donald and I can always build a little pen for them at the back of the inn. We've more room than you, and the hens can peck away there to their hearts' content. Or at least until this business is sorted out and they can go back to the shore as before.'

'Thanks, Hector,' smiled Jinty. 'You're a good soul. And I'm not the only one who thinks so. Don't let this Vladimir business get you down. We'll think of something.'

'I think I'd better get along and finish the making the pastry for the apple tarts,' said Kirsty. 'Or there will be nothing to go with the strawberry ice cream.'

There was a moment's silence while everybody mentally tasted Kirsty's apple tart with strawberry ice cream. Strawberry ice cream made with home grown strawberries and thick, clotted cream from a local farm. Then we left and went back to the inn.

Dad was thoughtful. 'Strange business, that, with these hens. I've never seen hens act like that before. Have you, Donald?'

Donald shook his head. 'They're usually placid enough creatures. Not especially bright, but not given to staggering about in the middle of the road.'

And that image struck me. That and the memory of my conga with the Lifeboat ladies. They had been staggering about too, then they had gone to sleep, just like the hens. There had to be a connection. Perhaps the eggs Constable Ross had taken away for analysis would give us the answer.

Chapter 18

I saw Ron Jackson again. Not out on the loch in the hotel's speedboat this time, but walking along the shore road with a stranger in a grey suit and a purple anorak. I was upstairs in my room, still wondering what I could contribute to the Grand Jumble Sale. I knew Morag was handing in her exercise bike. She said she never used it now, and it only made her feel guilty, sitting there in the corner of her bedroom, looking at her disapprovingly when she stuffed her face with a cream cake. Kirsty was donating the recorder she'd played in school.

'Would you maybe be thinking about donating your bagpipes too, Kirsty?' Henry McCrumble had asked hopefully.

'Certainly not,' said Kirsty. 'I need them to practise with. How else will I get into the Auchtertuie pipe band?'

Henry had muttered something about needing a miracle, but only when Kirsty was out of earshot.

I had wondered fleetingly about donating a cuddly toy from the pile on my bed. But which one? I looked at them all. Not the rhinoceros. I couldn't do that. I had bought him at the Grand Jumble Sale last year because no one else would. He looked so sad, sitting there on the toy stall on his own after all the other cuddlier toys had been sold, that I just had to buy him and take him home. He's an all-over pale grey velvet with two darker, rather squashed little horns. The insides of his ears are a tender pink. I called him Ringo. I'd like to go and see real rhinos in the wild some day. Ringo's best friend is a zebra called Spot. One of the guests left him in the lounge of the Crumbling Arms years ago, and I kept him in case they would come back for him, but they never did.

Then there's Goldilocks and the three bears. Four bears if you count baby bear's tiny teddy bear. Kirsty made me Goldilocks when I was little. She's a soft-bodied doll with a red and white checked dress, red apple cheeks and yellow wool hair tied up in bunches. Her hair fell off once, a bit like Vladimir's, but Kirsty sewed it back on. Father bear has lost an ear and mother bear has a patch on her right paw. Baby bear has a squint and doesn't look wise. But I love them all, so they couldn't go to the jumble sale either.

Who did that leave? Only Mac, the tartan Scotty dog, that an aunt of Dad's had given him when he was little. He has a frayed tail and a grumpy expression – the dog, that is. I suspect he keeps the other toys in order when I'm not around, so he couldn't go either. Looking out jumble is not easy.

I was just explaining this to the toys when I spotted Ron Jackson and his pal from my side window. I hurried into one of the empty guest bedrooms on the other side of the inn to get a closer look. By this time the men were on the shore side of the road, looking over at the Crumbling Arms. Ron Jackson seemed to be pointing out several things about the building while his pal in the suit and the anorak made notes.

'Now what's all that about?' I wondered. I went downstairs and into the kitchen. Dad was sitting at the big kitchen table, poring over some bills.

'Ron Jackson and another man are out front,' I said. 'They seem to be looking in a funny way at the Crumbling Arms.'

'Uh-huh,' said Dad, trying to make his figures add up.

'What do you think I should do?'

'Nothing, Kat. There's no law against looking. Even in a funny way.'

'But I'm sure they're up to something. Ron Jackson's always up to something and it's never anything good.'

'Look,' said Dad. 'Why don't you take the dogs out for some fresh air and stop worrying about Ron Jackson.'

'OK,' I grinned, as a thought struck. 'Good idea, Dad.' And I went and collected, not just Millie and Max, but Donk and Lily and Shampers too.

I often take the dogs and donkeys for a walk, so why not a ferret as well? He's really tame and friendly and well used to humans.

'Walkies, guys,' I said. 'Where would you like to go? Along the lochside?'

No one had a better idea so we left the back yard, went round the side of the Crumbling Arms and crossed the shore road. Samantha, who misses nothing, decided to join us, keeping well upwind of Shampers who was sitting on my shoulder, clinging to my old jersey like a real live cuddly toy.

By this time, Ron Jackson and his pal had their

heads together examining a large sheet of white paper, so we were almost upon them before they noticed us.

'What the—?' Ron Jackson started to say as Donk nudged past and stopped. 'Oh it's you, Kat McCrumble. You and your stupid animal menagerie. Animals on the public highway shouldn't be allowed.'

'They're not on the highway, they're on the lochside,' I said, 'and they're doing no harm.'

'Oh no, they're lovely,' said a woman in the little crowd which always started to gather whenever I appeared with the animals.

'What are the donkeys called?' asked a little boy.

'Donk and Lily.'

'What are the dogs called?' asked their mum, stooping to pat them.

'Millie's the sensible one. The one trying to eat your crisps is Max.'

'Does the ferret have a name?' asked a tall man. 'My dad used to keep ferrets. It's years since I stroked one.'

'He's called Shampers,' I said.

Ron Jackson snorted. 'Shampers, huh. Vermin more like.'

Now I don't know whether Shampers didn't like his tone, or, being a true polecat, objected to being called vermin, but he leapt off my shoulder and on to Ron Jackson's.

'Ow, get him off me,' Ron Jackson yelled, and made a grab for him, dropping the big white piece of paper.

But Shampers was too fast. He was up over the gamekeeper's head, flicking him on the face with his tail before dropping on to his other shoulder, running down his arm, and back to me.

'Yeugh, you'll pay for this, Kat McCrumble,' spat out Ron Jackson, 'just wait and see. I hate the smell of ferret.'

His pal backed away from him. He obviously didn't like the smell of ferret either.

I grinned. Anything that annoyed Ron Jackson was all right by me. And there was something else that annoyed him. Donk and Lily had trampled on, then started to eat, the big piece of white paper that had fallen to the ground.

I took it from them. 'Don't eat that,' I said. 'It's probably poisoned.'

Now I know I shouldn't have said that, but it just slipped out.

Ron Jackson gave me a hard stare. I gave him one right back and handed over the battered bit of paper. Then I wished I hadn't, for on the top corner I spotted something. The words 'Proposed

Renovations' leapt out at me, and underneath them, something else. An unmistakable drawing of the Crumbling Arms.

Chapter 19

My mind was in a whirl as I carried on along the lochside with the animals. People stopped me to ask about them. I don't really know what I said. I can only hope it sounded sensible. Donk and Lily gave some of the smaller children rides on their backs, and Shampers let them stroke his furry coat. Max raced into the water after a ball someone threw for him, then soaked everyone when he bounded back out and shook himself dry. Millie stayed with me, her head at my knee, constantly looking up at me. Millie always knows when something is wrong. I patted her head, then, after a while, took everyone home.

I settled the donkeys and Shampers back in their

homes and went to find Dad. He was still in the kitchen, poring over the accounts. I opened my mouth to tell him what had happened, then shut it again. It would only give Dad something else to worry about. So, I turned on my heel and went upstairs, Millie and Max at my side.

I hate having to just worry about things. I like being able to *do* something about them.

I made another mental list of the present problems and how I might be able to help.

Vladimir?

Nope. Dad was doing all he could looking for papers to prove we owned the Crumbling Arms. I wouldn't know where to start.

Ron Jackson/the man in the grey suit/Callum McCrumble?

Nope. Absolutely no proof of anything. Even I didn't need Constable Ross to tell me that.

Jinty's hens?

Constable Ross was already investigating. All I knew about eggs was that you could eat them, cook with them, or occasionally throw them at people you didn't like. Not that I would ever do that, of course!

The poisoned peregrines?

Now, wait a minute, perhaps there was something I could do about that.

'Fancy another walk?' I asked the dogs.

Silly question.

'Shall we sneak into the estate this time?'

They didn't have a better idea, so I put Max on his lead. Millie would be fine.

'Now listen,' I whispered to them. 'We're going on a top-secret mission. I don't know what it is we're looking for, just anything suspicious. OK?'

I didn't really expect to find a signed confession by Ron Jackson saying,

To whom it may concern,
I am the peregrine poisoner. Please inform Constable Ross immediately and ask him to lock me up.

Though that would be nice.

We slipped out through the front door, avoiding the kitchen and Dad, and went round the side of the Crumbling Arms, across the back yard and into the forest. It was light at the edge of the forest where the sunlight filtered through, but it soon became gloomier as we went further in. Millie stayed by my side, nose constantly to the ground. Max, as usual, tugged hard on his lead, almost pulling me over in his efforts to get away.

'Heel, Max,' I hissed.

I may as well have shouted 'elephants', but it was worth a try.

I like to go into the forest whenever I can. Donald has told me all about the different trees and shown me all the secret pathways he uses. I headed down one of them now, knowing it would take me to a high rocky area by the side of the Ben. An area where I knew the peregrines liked to nest. Dad and I had often seen them swooping backwards and forwards to a high ledge to feed a white fluffy chick. Peregrines on the lookout for prey are fascinating to watch. They remain high in the sky till they see what they want, usually a pigeon or a grouse, then they plummet towards it in a wind-whistling 'stoop', taking it in the air. That was what I couldn't understand about the poisoning. How was it getting into the peregrines?

I continued on the pathway, making as little noise as possible. Even so, scurryings in the undergrowth said our arrival had been noticed. A little deer leapt across our path at one point, scaring the socks off Max. He let out a yelp and started to bark, but I covered his muzzle with my hands and soothed him.

'It's all right, Max. It's all right. Just a little deer. Shush, now.'

Max looked like he might protest some more, so I searched in the pocket of my jeans and found half a dog biscuit. That helped a bit. Food always did with Max. I just hoped no one had heard him bark. I stayed still for a moment, listening, but the sounds all around us were normal forest sounds. I let out a long sigh, finding that I had been unconsciously holding my breath.

'Let's go,' I said.

We set off again, passing indigenous trees of birch, oak, mountain ash and alder. But these soon gave way to the conifers which had been planted in long, neat rows and now reached well up the lower slopes of the Ben. After a while I came to a spot I knew well and took a right fork. I knew this would bring me out to the craggy rock face where the peregrines lived.

'I don't expect I'll find anything,' I whispered to Millie. 'But at least I'll feel I'm doing something.'

Not long afterwards we came in sight of the rock face. I picked out a suitable spot and sat down with my back against a tree to watch – for what, I wasn't sure. Millie sat on my right and watched too. Max put his head on my feet and went to sleep.

After a while, when our presence had been accepted and the forest had settled around us, I spotted a peregrine. It was wheeling in the thermals above the cliff face.

'Look at that, Millie,' I whispered. 'Aren't they

beautiful birds? They don't deserve to be poisoned just for trying to survive. Just for trying to bring up their chicks.'

Millie's ears twitched. She was a good listener. Max's tail twitched. He was probably having a good dream. My nose twitched. It needed a good blow. I reached into my pocket for my hanky, but it was too late.

'*ATISHOO.*'

The sneeze wakened Max. He jumped up and took off before I could grab his lead.

'Max, come back,' I yelled, hoping no one was near enough to hear me.

Max heard me, but, as usual, paid no heed. Millie bounded after him. I bounded after her.

'Help,' I thought, 'if Max follows his nose like he usually does, we could end up on top of the Ben . . . and Dad would be furious because he's told me often enough how dangerous that is. And he'd be worried if I didn't get home pretty soon. And I should have told him where I was going. And, as usual, I should have thought of all this earlier. Oh well.'

Then I heard barking. That was Max. More barking. That was Millie. I followed the sound, hoping she had found Max. She had. Max had stopped in a little clearing. He had found something too. He was barking at something perched on top of a stake planted in the ground. I squinted up at it. What on earth . . . ? It was a dead pigeon.

'Oh,' I gasped, realisation dawning. I hadn't found out who was poisoning the peregrines, but now I was sure I had found out how.

I couldn't reach the top of the stake, but I managed to wiggle it enough for the pigeon to fall off. I got to it just before Max.

'Oh no, you don't,' I said. 'This is evidence. This is going right back to Constable Ross.'

And I held the poor thing by its claws and carried it home.

Chapter 20

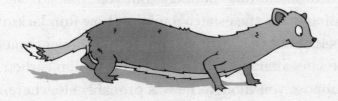

Dad took charge of the 'evidence' and put it in a poly bag. Then he sent me to have a good scrub up while he phoned Constable Ross. He hadn't said anything yet about my going into the estate without telling him, but I knew that particular row was still to come. I was just hoping I could plead finding the 'evidence', if that's what it turned out to be, as mitigating circumstances.

Constable Ross was on his tea break when he got Dad's call, but came over right away. I hurried downstairs to meet him.

'What's this I hear, Kat?' he said, following Dad into the lounge. 'Have you been doing my job again?' Then he sat down on the sofa, put his hat on the coffee table and listened intently to my story.

I told him what had happened as clearly as I could. 'I just wanted to feel I was doing something,' I finished up. 'And the pigeon might be evidence, mightn't it?'

Constable Ross nodded. 'But you took a chance going off to the estate. You know how Ron Jackson feels about that. Still, I suppose you thought you'd be safe, after the run-in you had with him earlier. I suppose you thought he was probably elsewhere.'

'What run-in?' said Dad. 'What's been going on?'

The Auchtertuie gossips had been going on, that's what.

'Och, I just went into the bakery to get an empire biscuit for my afternoon tea break,' said Constable Ross, 'and Jinty told me what she'd seen from the window. She said she couldn't hear what was going on, but by the expression on Ron Jackson's face, he wasn't best pleased with Kat or the animals.'

In spite of the fact that I knew Dad was annoyed, I grinned. 'Shampers leapt on to him and flicked his tail in his face, and Donk and Lily chewed up his plan of the Crumbling Arms.'

'What plan?' said Dad.

Oh dear. Me and my big mouth. So much for trying to keep a secret. So much for trying not to worry Dad.

I told them both what I had seen on the big piece of white paper.

Dad ran his fingers through his hair. 'What next?' he said.

Constable Ross stroked his chin. 'Aye, there's some funny goings on in Auchtertuie at the moment, right enough. But one thing at a time. Let's get the dead pigeon to the vet first and see what he says about it.'

Constable Ross picked up his hat and the pigeon and departed. That left Dad and me alone. I decided to get my apology in first. Sometimes that helps.

'Look, Dad, I know I should have told you I was going on to the estate, but you looked so worried about the accounts that I didn't want to worry you any further, and I wasn't going to tell you about the plans I saw on the white paper till I found out more about them. I know you've got lots of worries right now, and I was trying not to add to them, but I have, and I'm sorry. Really sorry.'

Dad just shook his head. 'You are my biggest worry, Kat. I can cope with all the others, but if anything happened to you . . .' And he left it there.

And, do you know something, I felt worse than if he'd given me a real bawling out.

Dad went into the bar to check the supplies for the evening rush and I wandered into the kitchen. Kirsty was there, busily preparing the evening meals.

'What's wrong with you, Kat McCrumble?' she said. 'You look like you've found a penny and lost a pound.'

'Just had a row from Dad,' I muttered.

'I didn't hear any yelling.'

'It wasn't that kind of row.'

'Oh, the more serious kind then.'

'Uh-huh.'

'Well,' said Kirsty, pushing up her sleeves. 'You have a choice. You can either mope about here like a moaning muppet or you can make yourself useful and divide that chocolate mousse into individual glasses for tonight's puddings . . . then scrape out the bowl and lick the spoon.'

Tough choice.

Licking the chocolate mousse spoon is one of my favourite occupations, so I was back to being cheerful when Morag came in to help Kirsty with the evening meals.

'Well, what do you think?' she said, pausing only to fasten on her big apron, with 'I love Auchtertuie' on the front. 'That Vladimir has been seen up at the big hotel.'

Kirsty stopped in the middle of her gravy stirring, and I stopped drying the lettuce I'd just washed. Everything stops for gossip in Auchtertuie.

'Henry McCrumble's wife, Lottie's, second cousin, Sarah?' asked Kirsty.

Morag nodded. 'She saw him pass the dining-room door and head for one of the lifts. He was in full Highland dress, so there was no mistaking him. Then one of the porters told her he went to the suite Callum McCrumble is in on the top floor. Now why would he be doing that do you think?'

'You tell us,' said Kirsty. 'You're the one with the second sight.'

'Aye, but there's not much coming through that makes a lot of sense at the moment,' said Morag.

'Nothing makes much sense at the moment,' I said, and told them about my encounter with Ron Jackson and the plans on the big piece of white paper. 'Unless ... unless, do you think Vladimir and Callum McCrumble could be in this business together? Trying to get hold of the Crumbling Arms, I mean?'

'It's a possibility ...' said Kirsty, then could say no more as her gravy boiled over and hissed on the stove top and she had to act fast to rescue it.

There was no time for any more discussion that evening as we were so busy, and when bedtime came, I fell into bed and slept soundly. I was just helping Dad clear away the breakfast things next morning when Morag arrived with the post.

'I hope there are no bills, Morag,' said Dad. 'If there are, just send them back and say I've left the country. Gone to Alaska. No, make that Antarctica. No, on second thoughts, make that the moon. That should be far enough away.'

Morag looked at Dad kindly. 'Och, there are no bills this morning, Hector,' she said. 'Just a letter.'

'And?' said Dad. 'What's your famous second sight telling you about the contents? Has someone left me a fortune? Have I won the lottery?'

'You never do the lottery, Dad,' I reminded him.

'True. So what's in the letter, Morag?'

Morag shook her head. 'I wish I could say it was good news, Hector, but I can't. I'm afraid it's not good news. Not good news at all.'

Chapter 21

Dad just shook his head and opened the letter. I watched anxiously as his face paled. He sat down at the kitchen table and ran his fingers through his hair till it practically stood on end.

'What?' I said. 'What is it?'

'It's from Vladimir's lawyers in Edinburgh. They say they've had an expert look at Vladimir's family tree and it seems to be genuine. They will now be proceeding with all speed to prove beyond doubt that Vladimir is the rightful owner of the Crumbling Arms and chieftain of the Clan McCrumble.'

'They can't do that,' I cried, and grabbed hold of the letter.

'It's complete and utter rubbish,' said Morag.

'Everyone knows that,' said Kirsty. 'There must be some mistake. Experts. Huh!'

'Vladimir's document must be a fake,' I cried. 'A counterfeit. A counterfeit fake!'

Dad shook his head. 'I don't think so. The copy I have looks genuine enough to me. Anyway, the lawyers are an old established firm with a reputation to maintain. They wouldn't be party to anything underhand.'

'Then we'll go and see them,' I said, 'and tell them they're wrong. That they may have made an honest mistake, but they're just plain wrong.'

'If only it were that simple, Kat,' sighed Dad. 'But nothing ever is. I'll keep searching through the old documents I have upstairs, but I don't think there's anything I've missed.' And Dad went off, his shoulders slumped and rounded with anxiety. I'd never seen him so worried before.

'There must be something that can be done,' I said to Kirsty and Morag, but they just shook their heads. I knew they wanted to help too. I knew they would have climbed Ben Bracken backwards on their hands and knees, if they thought it would have helped Dad.

I ground my teeth in frustration (sorry, Mr Walker – he's my dentist), called on Millie and Max, and walked them along to Tina's. She was helping her dad bubble-wrap some of his funnily shaped pots.

'Hi, Kat,' she said. 'I was just going to phone you. Do you fancy a trip to Edinburgh tomorrow? I'm going with Dad to help him deliver his pots and Mum's scarves to that big store in Princes Street that's going to sell them.'

I opened my mouth to say 'no'. I didn't want to leave Dad alone with all that was happening. But then I thought. Edinburgh? That was where Vladimir's lawyers hung out. I remembered seeing an Edinburgh address on their headed notepaper. A little plan began to form in my mind. It wasn't much of a plan and it probably wouldn't work, but at least I would feel I was doing something. You know how I hate not to be *doing* something.

So . . .

'Thanks, Tina. That would be great. I'd love to go to Edinburgh tomorrow.'

Once we were there I would tell her my plan. Meantime all I had to do was check on the lawyers' address . . .

It was easily done. When Dad was downstairs in the bar in the early evening, I sneaked along to his little office and looked out the lawyers' letter. I wrote down the address on a scrappy bit of paper and stuffed it into my jeans pocket. So far so good.

Then I told Dad about my trip to Edinburgh. He was pleased.

'Do you good to get away for the day, Kat,' he said, and, even though I knew he couldn't afford it, he gave me some extra pocket money to spend in the capital.

Tina's dad, David, picked me up early next morning.

'It'll take us about four hours,' he said, as I climbed into the back of his old red estate car beside Tina. 'But Terri has made us up some sandwiches for the journey.'

'So has Kirsty,' I said.

'We'll eat hers,' whispered Tina, 'and dump Mum's when Dad's not looking.'

Both Tina and I had brought along some Abandon Hope CDs and her dad slipped them into the CD player and we settled down. It wasn't a fast journey. Tina's dad had to be careful with the bubble-wrapped pots in the back. I didn't mind. I had Tina to chat to, the music to listen to and my secret plan to mull over. I would tell Tina about it when we got to Edinburgh.

We passed through Fort William then headed on through Glencoe. It looked less sinister than usual in the bright sunlight. Then it was over Rannoch

Moor to Crianlarich and along the long road past Ben More. After that we headed down Glen Ogle to Lochearnhead and along Loch Earn to the beautiful city of Perth. From there, we took the motorway to Edinburgh and went across the magnificent Forth road bridge and into the city.

As always, Edinburgh was busy. It has even more tourists than Auchtertuie! Actually, I felt like a tourist myself as I craned my neck to look at the castle and the Scott monument. I had seen them before, of course, but I still wanted to look. I don't get to Edinburgh that often, and it's definitely much grander than Auchtertuie.

We got to the big store in Princes Street where Tina's dad had to deliver his pots. A commissionaire directed us round the corner to a private car park at the rear of the store.

'Look,' said Tina's dad, manoeuvring the red estate into a very small space, 'it's going to take me ages to unload this stuff and get all the paperwork sorted out, so why don't you two go off and have a look at the shops? Then meet me back here in a couple of hours?'

That was exactly what I was going to suggest. Only I didn't want to look at the shops.

We said 'cheerio' to Tina's dad, and, as soon as we were out of earshot, I told her my plan.

'I want to go and see Vladimir's lawyer,' I said, 'to see if I can find out anything more. See, I have his address,' and I fished the bit of paper out of my jeans. 'Do you want to come with me?'

Tina hesitated only for a second. 'Does your dad know?' she asked.

I gave a non-committal shrug.

'Then I'd better come and try to keep you out of trouble,' she sighed.

I gave her a hug and we headed for the nearest taxi rank. The extra pocket money Dad had given me would be useful, just not in the way he had thought. Fortunately, the lawyers' office was not far away, and I had plenty of money left over for the journey back.

The office was housed in an imposing grey building with glass swing doors. Tina and I went through, our trainers squeaking loudly on the polished wooden floor. That's when dragon lady looked up from her desk. Dragon lady had scraped-back, cinder-grey hair, large glasses and an expression not unlike Samantha's at her snootiest.

'Can I help you, young ladies?' she asked, in a voice that suggested it would be over her dead body if she did.

'How kind. You must be . . . Brenda McTaggart,' I said, scanning the name she had just signed at the bottom of a letter. Did I tell you I can read upside down? It's a great skill to have, especially in school. I find out all sorts of things. 'Uncle Ian, er, Mr White, said you would direct us to his office. We phoned him at home this morning to say we would be in town. We're hoping he might take us out for lunch.'

OK. I know it was a complete fabrication, a tremendous tarradiddle, a whopping great lie, in fact. But what else was I to do? How else was I going to get to see the lawyer? Thank goodness I had remembered his name from the letter.

Brenda McTaggart alias dragon lady looked undecided, but I put on my most winning, totally irresistible smile.

'Second floor on the left,' she said.

I thanked her warmly and we escaped upstairs.

'You are such a fibber, Kat McCrumble,' said Tina. 'How do you manage to lie with such a straight face?'

'Practice,' I grinned.

We soon found the door to 'Uncle Ian's' office suite and went inside. Oh no, another desk and another dragon lady. Except this one wasn't. This one was really nice.

'Hullo, girls,' she smiled. 'Don't you look fantastic in those skinny jeans? I wish I could squeeze myself into a pair, but there's no chance.' And she patted her ample rump. 'I'm Eilidh. What can I do for you?'

And do you know something? I couldn't lie to her. She had such an open face and kind smile that I found myself taking a deep breath and telling her the true story.

Eilidh listened carefully. 'Och that's terrible,' she said. 'I see your problem. Trouble is, Mr White is with a client at the moment, and I really can't disturb him. But I know who you're talking about. I shouldn't be telling you this, but that Vladimir McCrumble person came here. Dressed in full Highland regalia, he was. I thought at first he must have left his pipe band outside. But he wasn't alone, there was another man with him. Strange character, wore a dark suit and sunglasses. Never took them off. I don't like that. You can tell a lot about people from their eyes, and, if they don't show them, I reckon they're hiding something.'

I nodded in agreement, then I frowned. Something was familiar, nagging at my memory. I trawled swiftly back through the last few days. I had it. Sunglasses man. He had eaten in the Crumbling Arms. He had been here with Vladimir.

'You don't happen to know the other man's name?' I said.

'Oh yes,' said Eilidh. 'His name was McCrumble too. Callum McCrumble. I remember because Callum's my son's name.'

'Callum McCrumble,' I muttered. 'I was right. He is in cahoots with Vladimir.'

I thanked Eilidh and we left, smiling sweetly at dragon lady on the way out.

'Don't we need to see "Uncle Ian" now?' asked Tina.

I shook my head. 'I've got some more information now that I'll have to think about.'

And do you know, I thought about it all the way out of Edinburgh and all the way back to Auchtertuie, but I still didn't know exactly what it meant, how useful it was, or what I could do with it.

Chapter 22

One thing I could do was tell Dad, and I did that after we had served the breakfasts next morning. He was loading the plates into the dishwasher when I kind of slipped it into the conversation.

'That's the last of the cups from the dining room, Dad,' I said, 'and, by the way, I popped in to see Vladimir's lawyer when I was in Edinburgh yesterday.'

Dad paused, eggy breakfast plate in hand. 'You did what?'

'Well, I was passing, sort of. In a taxi,' I added, under my breath, so it wasn't too much of a lie. 'I didn't get to see the lawyer, but guess what . . . I met his secretary. She's called Eilidh and is very nice. She told me . . .' and I proceeded to tell Dad what I had found out.

Dad slotted the eggy plate into the dishwasher, frowned, but listened quietly.

When he had heard the story, he was both annoyed and pleased at the same time. Annoyed that I had gone to the lawyers' office without telling him, but pleased about what I had found out.

'Though I'm not quite sure yet how it helps, Kat,' he said.

'Me neither, except we know now who we're up against. Do you think Callum McCrumble has planned this whole thing? Do you think Vladimir's a fake?'

Dad shook his head. 'Unless I'm very much mistaken, Vladimir is genuine enough. There are McCrumbles all over the world. Some of them in eastern Europe. We've had visits from one or two before now.'

'But none that thought he was the rightful clan chief of the McCrumbles,' I said. 'None that came to claim the Crumbling Arms as his own.'

Dad nodded. 'If only I could find positive proof of our claim to the Crumbling Arms. I searched again while you were in Edinburgh, but no luck. What we really need is Old Hamish's father's will, stating that the castle and the land were left to Old

Hamish, as he was the elder twin. But we don't have that.'

Dad went back to loading the dishwasher. I put the breakfast butter dishes back into the fridge, just as Millie and Max shot past me and headed out into the back yard for their morning biscuit. Their keen ears had picked up the sound of the post van arriving.

'Morag's surely early this morning,' said Dad.

'No, she's not,' I said, looking at my watch. 'Kirsty's late.'

At that moment, Kirsty came hurrying in from the front hall. Her hair was wild, her eyes were wild and she was clearly furious.

'You'll never guess what's happened,' she said. 'Some . . . some . . . idiot spray-painted my front garden black.'

'What?'

'My beautiful white roses, my pink carnations, my lovely little lilac tree, all sprayed with horrible black paint,' she said, and her voice shook with anger. Kirsty's garden is her pride and joy and is much admired in Auchtertuie.

'How awful,' I gasped. 'Who would do such a thing?'

'Who knows?' said Kirsty. 'There are some very strange people in the world.'

Then Morag, accompanied by Millie and Max, came in from the back yard.

'Oh Kirsty,' said Morag, hurrying to give her a hug. 'I thought what happened to me was bad, but your lovely garden . . . I saw it on my way past. I'll help you clean it up. Have you any idea who did it?'

'No,' said Kirsty, 'but whoever it was had better hope Constable Ross catches them before I do. It's taken me years to get my garden the way I wanted it, and now it's all ruined. But,' Kirsty frowned, 'what do you mean . . . what happened to you?'

Morag sighed. 'You know the little collection of Snow White and the seven dwarves that sits outside my front door?'

We all nodded.

'All smashed in the night,' she said, her eyes a little moist.

'Smashed?' I cried. 'But they were lovely. I used to play with them when I was little.'

'So did all the other village children.' Dad's voice was grim. 'What's going on?'

Before we could hazard a guess, the back door banged open and Donald strode in. His face was as white as his frock and I had never seen him so angry.

'Someone has just hacked large lumps out of my oak tree,' he said.

'Your oak tree!' I was incredulous. It actually didn't belong to Donald. But I knew the one he meant. It was really old and gnarled and looked like it had come straight out of a fairy tale book, and it was the one Donald most liked to perch in.

'I was just going along to sit in it,' said Donald, 'when I saw the damage that had been done. There were branches torn off and great chunks cut out of it. There was a large axe lying nearby. I had just picked it up to take it to Constable Ross when Ron Jackson sprang out of the bushes. He grabbed the axe from me and said *he* was going to take it to Constable Ross and have me charged with malicious damage. As if I would ever do that to an oak tree. Or to any tree.'

'Of course, you wouldn't.' I ran to give him a hug. 'Everyone knows that.'

Dad ran his fingers through his hair, his expression grim. 'There's something really nasty going on here,' he said. 'I'm sure of it. First Vladimir tries to force us out of the Crumbling Arms and now you're all being targeted too.'

'And Callum McCrumble's definitely involved in it,' I said, and told the others about my discovery in Edinburgh.

Kirsty was apoplectic. 'You mean that man was in here and ate my food. That I actually cooked for him. And he spray-painted my garden. Just let me get my hands on him.'

'I'd like to get hold of him too,' said Morag. 'Poor Snow White. Poor little dwarves. Though I don't suppose Callum McCrumble would have smashed them up himself. These people always order others to do their dirty work.'

'And what sort of person attacks an old tree?' Donald shook his head sadly, but he was far too gentle to lay hands on anyone.

'Is Callum McCrumble still in his suite at the big hotel?' I asked innocently. But not innocently enough.

'Katriona McCrumble,' said Dad. 'We are in enough trouble as it is without you getting into any more. I absolutely forbid you to go anywhere near the big hotel.'

Pity.

Chapter 23

Emily, the tarantula, went home today. Her owner, Peter Parton, came with his dad to collect her. Peter's about two years younger than me and is tall and gangly, with thick dark hair just like his dad's. As it was a fine day, his dad was wearing shorts, so his dark hairy legs were on view too. They immediately reminded me of Emily's, though Mr Parton didn't have quite so many. Perhaps people do get to look like their pets after all, but, just before you start to wonder, no, I don't have huge ears like Donk, or a wet, black nose like Max, though I am sane and sensible like Millie.

Did I hear a snort of disbelief just then?

Tina came over with Micky, who nearly wagged

his tail off when he saw me. He's a really happy dog since he went to live with Tina and her family. I called to Millie and we took Mrs Tiggywinkle from her cage, put her into a shoe box, and went over to Henry McCrumble's house. Henry has a large safe garden, well away from the main road. We opened the creaking iron gate, wandered up the gravel path and pressed the doorbell. It plays a selection of Scottish tunes. 'A Hundred Pipers' whined out, failing to sound like even one piper.

'Hi, Kat. Hi, Tina,' said Henry, opening the door. 'No need to ask why you've come.'

I grinned. Henry's used to me appearing with shoe boxes full of rescued hedgehogs. 'No need at all,' I said.

We went through the house and out into the back garden. It's delightfully untidy with plenty of brushwood, compost and piles of leaves that make good hedgehog nests.

'Now stay in the garden and don't go near the traffic,' I cautioned Mrs Tiggywinkle as I handed her over to Henry.

'I'll have to put a Hedgehog B&B sign up outside soon, Kat McCrumble, if you bring me any more,' Henry tried to grumble.

But I just laughed. Henry loves hedgehogs. He now has several of them in his back garden. He keeps them supplied with plenty of caterpillars, slugs and snails, as well as putting out tinned cat food and muesli for them most evenings. But he doesn't put out bread and milk. That gives hedgehogs diarea . . . diahrea . . . diaryha . . . Oh help. It gives them the runs!

Most hedgehogs are killed on the roads at night, when they're out and about and at their most active. So, if you're out in a car at night, please be on hedgehog alert and get the driver to slow down. That's why I'd like to put up a sign or paint hedgehogs on the road, just to remind people.

You'll have noticed that I didn't take Max to Henry's house. Max isn't good with hedgehogs. He can't quite understand that, although they can roll themselves up, they don't actually like being used as a football. Or a pawball. Or a noseball. Max tried to play with a hedgehog once, but only once. He soon discovered that hedgehog spines up the nose are not very nice. That's why I left him at home with Dad and Donald. They were busy in the back yard making a run for Jinty's chickens. The chickens had now stopped laying and Jinty was convinced it was because they were in a huff at being kept indoors.

When we got back the new run was progressing well, despite Max's efforts to dodge away with Dad's hammer whenever he put it down.

'Oh hullo, you two,' smiled Dad, when he saw us. 'You're just in time to hold up the roll of chicken wire while I nail it to the posts.'

Tina and I helped unroll the wire and the run was almost complete when Constable Ross came round the side of the inn and into the back yard. He was wearing his policeman's hat and a very official expression.

'Ah good,' he said, coming over. 'This'll be the new chicken run. I'm glad you're taking Jinty's chickens for they may have to be kept away from the shoreline for some time.'

'Have you found out why they acted so strangely?' I asked. 'Was there something in the eggs?'

Constable Ross nodded. 'The analysis of the eggs came back. There was some evidence of drugs in them.'

'Drugs?' said Dad. 'Oh no. I'd hoped we had managed to keep Auchtertuie free of drugs.'

Donald just shook his head sadly. He has his own little world of trees and animals and the goings on in the outside world mystify him sometimes.

'But how did the hens get the drugs?' asked Tina.

'Simple,' I said. 'They peck along the lochside, they must have eaten something that's been washed up. Probably from Vladimir's boat.'

Constable Ross nodded. 'I searched the shoreline

and found some plastic bags containing white powder. The hens had obviously been pecking at them.'

I got excited. 'Does that mean you can go out to the boat and arrest everyone? Bring them ashore and lock them up. I could help you tackle Vladimir, if you like. I'm good at that. We've been playing girls' rugby at school. I could help you handcuff him too. I'd like that.'

Constable Ross patted my arm. 'Slow down, Kat,' he said. 'I know how you feel about Vladimir, but there's the small matter of proof.'

'Oh that,' I said. 'But it's obvious where the drugs are coming from.'

'Maybe. We shall have to find out. I have some colleagues arriving shortly from Fort William with a search warrant. They'll help me search the boat.'

'Then you'll have to go in disguise.' I was getting really enthusiastic about this operation. 'You can't all head out there in your policemen's uniforms or they'll see you coming and throw any proof over the side.'

'Now why didn't I think of that?' Constable Ross shook his head. 'Why didn't I think to hire Lachy McCrumble's boat and have him ready to cast off the minute my *plain clothes* colleagues get here?'

'Right,' I grinned. Maybe our policeman knew a

thing or two after all. Maybe he watched the same cop shows on television I do.

Constable Ross left and Tina and I took up residence on the window seat in the lounge and kept a lookout. After a little while we saw a group of 'tourists' go on board Lachy's old fishing smack. Then Lachy cast off and headed out towards Vladimir's boat. There was a fair wind and the loch was quite choppy. I hoped all the policemen were good sailors.

'Oh, I wish I could be with them,' I said to Tina. 'I hate being stuck here while something's going on.'

'But it *is* exciting,' said Tina. 'Do you think they'll find anything?'

'I don't know,' I said, and thought of the Lifeboat ladies dancing up and down the lounge and Jinty's hens dancing in the street. Then I remembered how Vladimir's sailors had been dancing that time I'd gone out to the boat, but dancing's hardly a crime. I did know that without any absolute proof it would be difficult for Constable Ross to do anything at all. Just as we were finding it difficult to stop Vladimir doing exactly what he wanted about the Crumbling Arms. I gave a deep sigh. Why is life so difficult sometimes? Why is it so unfair? Why do the bad guys get away with things?

I looked around the lounge with its shabby chairs and squinty pictures, and the old Robert Burns firescreen covering the fallen-down chimney stones. The Crumbling Arms wasn't a palace, but it was home. Home to me and Dad. There was just no way Vladimir could be allowed to have it. No way at all.

Chapter 24

It was late before Constable Ross came back. Tina and Micky had gone home, and, to keep my mind off things, I had helped Kirsty with the dinners. Dad and I were just clearing up the last of the dishes when he appeared in the kitchen. One look at his face told us the news.

'You found something?' I grinned.

Constable Ross placed several bags of white powder on the table. 'Evidence,' he said.

'Then you can clap Vladimir and his crew in irons,' I said happily. 'The good guys win at last. That'll get Vladimir off our backs.'

But Constable Ross shook his head. 'I don't think Vladimir had any knowledge of the drugs, Kat. He hates them and regularly inspects the boat to make sure there are none aboard. But, in his searches, he didn't inspect the galley properly. We discovered the drugs, hidden in plain sight, in a jar marked, "Baking Powder". The cook was the drug dealer, regularly supplying several members of the crew. They were happy to tell us all about it rather than be arrested. Apparently Vladimir had had a snap inspection last week and they'd had to throw their packets of powder overboard or be caught. That's what washed ashore and what the hens found and pecked at. It affected them, their eggs and also the cake that the Lifeboat ladies ate.'

'Hmm.' The mystery was solved, but I refused to be impressed. 'So you can't arrest Vladimir then?'

'Only the cook.'

I folded my arms and put on my mutinous expression. 'Are you sure . . . ?'

Dad frowned at me. 'A good result, Willie,' he said. 'Well done.' Then he quickly changed the subject. 'The chicken run is finished. We can move Jinty's hens in tomorrow.'

Constable Ross, now biting into a leftover slice of apple tart, nodded. 'Just till I make sure no more drugs are still likely to be washed ashore.'

'What about my garden and Morag's figurines?' said Kirsty.

'And that business with Ron Jackson and Donald?' I said. 'Donald's really worried.'

'I told Ron Jackson the axe wasn't much good as evidence as it had his fingerprints on it as well as Donald's,' said Constable Ross, wiping his sticky fingers on a nearby tea towel. 'So Donald needn't worry about that. It's you folks who have to worry. There's obviously a campaign being mounted against you to get you out of the Crumbling Arms, and part of that campaign is to try to scare away the people who work for you. But the organiser or organisers are clever. They leave no clues. Nothing for me to go on. You must just be careful. All of you.' And Constable Ross picked up his evidence and left.

Kirsty went home soon after, and Dad and I were left alone.

'What are we going to do, Dad?' I asked.

Dad just shook his head. 'I don't know, Kat, and talking about it won't help either. Why don't you go up to bed now? You worked hard tonight, you must be tired out.'

I gave Dad a hug and trudged upstairs, followed by Millie and Max. Millie sensed I was worried and stayed close to me. Max, as usual, bounded up the stairs ahead of us and hurried to my bedroom. He would be up on my bed and pretending to be fast asleep by the time I got there. Millie reached the top of the stairs just before me. She turned to face me, then stiffened. Her tail drooped, her ears went flat and a little whine escaped from her throat.

'What is it, Millie?' I turned to look back down the stairs. There, in the downstairs hall, just hovering by the door of the lounge, was Old Hamish. He was looking up at me, his face anxious, his arm outstretched.

'It's all right, Millie.' I patted her head. 'It's Old Hamish. He means no harm. Maybe he's come to help. Maybe he's come to tell me something.' I started back down the stairs towards him, but the kitchen door opened and Dad came out along the hallway on his way to lock up. Old Hamish disappeared.

'Hamish,' I called. 'Don't go. Dad, did you see him? Did you see Old Hamish? He was just there by the lounge door. Surely you saw him?'

Dad looked up at me. 'I saw no one, Kat,' he said quietly. 'There was no one there to see. You're just over-anxious with all that's going on. Now go to bed and try to get some sleep.'

'But Old Hamish was there . . .' I started to say, but Dad was already locking the front door and throwing over the rusty bolts that we had never had to use before.

I trailed along to my bedroom with Millie. 'You saw him, Millie. I know you did. You saw Old Hamish. I'm sure he was coming to see me. I'm sure he was trying to help.'

Millie leaned her comforting weight on my leg, then sat on guard at the door of my room till I was safely in bed. The bed, of course, was already occupied by Max, feigning sleep.

'Down, Max,' I said.

Max opened one eye and gave me his 'do you mean me?' look.

'Down,' I repeated.

He gave a deep sigh and scrambled off the bed.

I slid under my duvet and worried. Dimly I heard the telephone ring downstairs as a pale moon came out from behind a cloud and made strange shadows on my bedroom wall. I shivered. There were too many shadows in my life at the moment, so I closed my eyes tightly, pulled the duvet over my head, and eventually fell asleep.

Chapter 25

Dad got ready to leave soon after we had finished the breakfasts next morning.

'Cash and carry?' I asked.

'No, just one or two things to do,' he replied vaguely.

'Probably gone to see Jinty about bringing over her hens,' I told Kirsty when she arrived later with the shopping.

'Look, Kat,' said Kirsty. 'Why don't you have the day off today? We're not too busy and you've been helping out a lot recently. I can manage fine.'

'OK,' I grinned. I didn't need to be told twice. I phoned Tina and she came over with Micky.

'Hi, Kat,' she said, when I met her at the front

door. 'What are we going to do today? Any ideas?'

Oh yes. I had been thinking and I knew exactly what I wanted to do.

'Fancy walking the dogs through the estate by the big hotel?' I said innocently.

Tina wasn't fooled. 'Kat, you know your dad has forbidden you to go anywhere near Callum McCrumble.'

'Wouldn't be going anywhere near him,' I said. 'The hotel has a huge garden and we would be on the estate over the boundary fence from that.'

'But why?' said Tina. 'Why risk getting into more trouble? What good would it do?'

'Do you remember how we went on to the estate when Abandon Hope were staying there? How we hoped we'd meet them taking a stroll?'

'Of course, and we found Micky instead. I'll never forget it.'

'Well, Callum McCrumble has to stretch his legs too, hasn't he? He doesn't walk into the village, probably knows he wouldn't be that welcome, so he may just walk around the estate instead. It's possible.'

'It's possible,' said Tina, 'but unlikely. I doubt we would bump into him.'

'Then there would be no harm in going, would there?'

Tina shook her head. 'You tricked me, Kat McCrumble. You are a very devious person.'

'Does that mean you'll come?' I grinned.

'Yes, but only to try to keep you out of trouble.'

I called the dogs, and, when Kirsty wasn't looking, we slipped out across the back yard. Donk and Lily lifted their heads in 'hullo', but I put my finger to my lips and they went back to nuzzling each other. It's their favourite occupation.

We entered the wood at the back of the Crumbling Arms and headed in the direction of the estate.

'Are you sure we're not breaking the law, Kat?' Tina was anxious.

'No, we're doing no harm. Just out for a walk with the dogs. I'll put Max on his lead when we get near to the hotel gardens, so he doesn't make a sudden mad dash for the swimming-pool. That would certainly give us away. It's really good that Dad's away today, it lets me feel I'm doing something about our problems without worrying him.'

'Hmm . . .'

I don't think Tina was convinced.

We trudged on through the forest. I took the

secret paths that Donald had shown me when I was little, though at times I think Tina was convinced there was no path at all.

'Kat, are you sure you know where we're going?'

'Trust me,' I grinned, and motioned her to be still when we came across a pile of hazelnut shells at the foot of a tree. A hazelnut shell fell at my feet and I pointed upwards.

Tina looked and took a deep breath. 'A red squirrel,' she whispered.

I nodded. 'Having a late breakfast. Usually they eat early morning and evening.'

We went on quietly, leaving the squirrel to his meal. After a while we came to the boundary fence that separated the hotel garden from the rest of the estate.

'You did know where you were going after all,' said Tina.

'Yep,' I grinned, and put the lead on Max, who had his rear end stuck up in the air as he investigated a rabbit burrow. He gave me a seriously miffed look. We walked on, keeping to the shelter of the trees, so as not to be visible to any of the hotel guests who might be strolling in the garden. I gazed hard at any I saw in the distance, but none of them looked like sunglasses man. I was sure of that. I had worked out what our route would be through the estate, but I hadn't worked out what I would say to Callum McCrumble if I did meet him. I would worry about that if it happened. Somehow I didn't think my tongue would desert me.

Suddenly Millie tensed. She had heard something further into the forest. Tina and I stood very still and listened. Millie and Micky stood still too. Max strained at his lead, trying to get away.

'Go on, Millie,' I whispered. 'Lead us to whoever it is.'

Delicately Millie picked her way over tree roots and led us deeper into the forest. I shortened Max's lead and followed on. Micky brought up the rear with Tina. After a while, Millie stopped abruptly. We had come to a little clearing. But there was nothing there except a pile of brushwood under one of the trees. Millie looked puzzled. She was obviously sure she had heard something, but now it was eerily quiet. No tiny animals rustling in the undergrowth, no birds calling from the trees. No sound at all till . . .

'Katriona McCrumble, what are you doing here?'

I nearly jumped out of my socks. I wheeled round. There was only one person that could be.

'Dad,' I gasped. 'What are YOU doing here?'

'I asked you first.'

Oops.

Fortunately I was saved from replying by Donald

and Constable Ross appearing from behind some nearby trees.

'What's going on?' I asked.

'We were hoping to catch the peregrine poisoner,' said Dad.

'You think he's been here?'

'Pretty sure of it,' said Donald. 'I was walking through this way last night, just before the light failed, and I found a lot of pigeon feathers on the ground.'

'But there are lots of wood pigeons around here,' I said.

Donald nodded. 'But I also found a torn label from a bottle containing the poison that killed the peregrines.'

'Wow. Does that help?'

'A bit,' said Constable Ross, 'but it's not quite enough. It could have been blown here, for example. I phoned your dad and the three of us came out here this morning looking for the bad guys, but so far all we've come up with is you two.'

'Sorry, it was my idea. It's all my fault,' I said, realising I had just made things worse. 'Are we contaminating a crime scene?'

'Probably not,' said Constable Ross. 'We've had a good look round, but I don't think there's anything else to be learned.'

At that moment, Max, sensing my attention was elsewhere, tugged his lead out of my hand and took off. I just saw the white scut of a rabbit disappear under the pile of brushwood as Max chased after it.

'Leave it alone, Max,' I shouted, as I chased after him. But half of Max's body had disappeared under the pile of dry branches, and no amount of coaxing would bring him out till he had got what he wanted. Finally he slithered out backwards, holding in his mouth, not the expected rabbit, but a red plastic bottle.

'Give it here, Max,' I said, and, pulling my sleeve down over my fingers to avoid getting my prints on the bottle, I gently prised the D-shaped handle from his jaws.

I looked at the torn label on the bottle and grinned. 'Good boy, Max,' I said. 'Good boy.'

Max looked pleased and wagged his tail. He didn't know what he had done, but he looked pleased anyway.

I carried the red plastic bottle back to the others. 'Does this help?' I said, handing it to Constable Ross.

He slipped his hand into a polythene evidence bag and took it from me. He looked at the label and smiled. 'Oh yes, Kat. It matches the label

Donald brought to the station. This helps quite a bit. I'll have it checked for fingerprints and see what we can come up with.'

Chapter 26

Dad disappeared off really early next morning too.

'You're not sneaking on to the estate again, are you?' I grinned.

'No,' he said. 'I leave that to you, Kat. I have an early appointment with the bank manager in Fort William. I'm going to see if he'll lend us some money.'

'To fight Vladimir in court?'

Dad nodded. 'It's all we can do. We can't just roll over and play dead because he says this place is his.'

'But you hate borrowing money,' I said. 'And we've only just finished paying for the roof to be fixed after last autumn's gales.'

'I know,' said Dad, 'and I've gone round it in my head a million times, but there's no other way.'

And he left, his face set in a worried expression.

I was worried too, but that soon turned to anger as I thought about what Vladimir had done to us. He may have seemed like a figure of fun to begin with, but he was obviously deadly serious about putting us out of the Crumbling Arms and becoming clan chief. What I didn't understand was where Callum McCrumble fitted into all of this. If he was in cahoots with Vladimir, as we thought, what was in it for him? We already knew how much he wanted the Crumbling Arms for himself. But if Vladimir became the owner, had he then agreed to sell it to Callum McCrumble? I wasn't sure. Somehow I didn't think so. He had genuinely seemed to want the inn for himself. We get a lot of people from all over the world visiting us to find out about their family roots, and we know how important it is to them. Like Dad, I turned the problem over and over in my head till my brain ached. But I was still no further forward. I rammed the last of the breakfast dishes into the dishwasher and slammed the door shut so hard the dishes rattled. Samantha appeared round the kitchen door to find out what all the noise was about.

'It's just not fair, Samantha,' I said. 'It's just not fair.'

And do you know, Samantha came and rubbed her head against my leg. Even she seemed to sense how desperate things now were.

I was just stroking her pointy little ears when Kirsty arrived.

'You'll never guess what's happened, Kat,' she said, dumping the shopping on the kitchen table.

'Probably not,' I said. I was in no mood for guessing games.

Kirsty didn't notice, she was so full of her news.

'This was through my letterbox when I came downstairs this morning. It must have been delivered by hand in the night.' And she handed me a letter. 'Read it out,' she commanded, 'so I know my eyes aren't deceiving me.'

I unfolded the letter and read.

Dear Ms McCrumble,
It has come to my attention that your beautiful garden has been vandalised by a person or persons unknown. I have often admired the garden and was sorry to hear that such an asset to the village had been damaged. I have arranged for my head gardener to call on you and discuss any replacement plants you might need. This will be at no expense to you. I hope

162

to see your garden in full bloom again before
too long.
Yours sincerely,
Callum McCrumble.

'I don't believe it,' I cried. 'After all this time,
and all the dirty tricks he's played, he's decided to
take a sudden interest in the village. He's up to
something.'

'That's what I thought,' said Kirsty, 'but what?'

'Dunno.' I shook my head. My brain was still in
meltdown.

The arrival of Morag with the post didn't help
much either.

'You'll never guess what's happened,' she said,
dumping herself down on a chair at the kitchen
table.

'Here we go again,' I sighed. 'You've not had a
letter from Callum McCrumble too?'

'How did you know that?' Morag was amazed. 'I
do the second sight bit around here, remember?'

'I had a letter too,' said Kirsty, 'but tell us about
yours.'

'It was through my letterbox when I came
downstairs this morning. It must have been
delivered by hand sometime in the night.'

Does any of this seem familiar to you?

'Tell us what was in your letter.'

'Only an offer to replace my Snow White and the seven dwarves figures. Seems Callum McCrumble had admired them and was sorry to hear they'd been damaged. I'm to expect a delivery of some new figures soon.'

'At absolutely no cost to you,' I snorted.

'Kat, are you sure you're not developing the second sight? Have you been seeing anything strange recently . . . any visions?'

I shook my head. 'Tell her, Kirsty,' I said.

Kirsty relayed what was in her letter.

'Well, who'd have thought it?' said Morag. 'I wonder what Callum McCrumble's up to.'

We were still wondering when Donald came in, looking a bit puzzled.

'Don't tell me,' I said. 'You've had a letter.'

He nodded and took it from a concealed pocket in his white frock. 'It seems I'm to expect a delivery of new trees to plant wherever I wish on the estate. It seems that my care of the trees on the estate has not gone unnoticed.'

'And it's signed Callum McCrumble, right?' I said.

Donald nodded. 'What's going on? What's he up to?'

'Perhaps he gave the orders for all the damage

that's been done, just so he could now appear to be really friendly and trying to help. Just so he could appear to be a really nice guy.'

'It's possible,' said Morag.

'It's probable,' sniffed Kirsty.

'But to damage an old tree, and someone's garden, and the toys that the children play with,' said Donald. 'What kind of person does that?'

'The kind I would like to catch,' said Constable Ross, appearing at the kitchen door.

We had been so engrossed in our discussion we hadn't heard his size twelves arrive.

'But I have some good news,' he grinned. 'And this is all down to Kat and Max.'

Max heard his name and wagged his tail.

'I had the poison bottle we recovered yesterday dusted for fingerprints, and a good friend who owes me a favour immediately ran the fingerprints through the police computer. Guess whose came up as a match?'

That was an easy one. 'Ron Jackson,' I cried.

'The very same,' said Constable Ross. 'His fingerprints were on file. Seems he's been in trouble before . . . for malicious damage.'

'So you can lock him up and throw away the key,' I said happily.

'No, Kat.' Constable Ross was patient. 'But it does

give me something to go on with the damage that was done to Kirsty's garden and the figurines and the old tree, and, of course, he'll be charged with poisoning the peregrines and appear in court. But I doubt he'll get much more than a fine for that, which will probably be paid by the estate, as he and Callum McCrumble seem to be as thick as thieves. There's just not enough account taken of wildlife crime, in my opinion, but, there it is, at least we've caught him.'

'That's good,' I said. 'And if it stops him . . .'

And we were still talking about wildlife crime when Dad arrived back from Fort William.

I ran to tell him. 'Ron Jackson's fingerprints were on the bottle. We've caught him at last. But you're back quickly, Dad. What did the bank manager say?'

'The bank manager said "no",' said Dad, and slumped down into a chair. 'Apparently the Crumbling Arms is just not a good enough risk for the bank to lend us more money. Especially since we'd be no better off, even if we won the case and sent Vladimir packing.'

'Oh,' I said, and put my arms round his shoulders.

Dad patted my hand. 'Try not to worry, Kat. Something will turn up.'

Morag clucked sympathetically and stood up to

go. 'Oh, I nearly forgot,' she said. 'There's a letter for you, Hector.'

'I hope it's good news,' said Kirsty, and looked at Morag, but Morag just gave a slight shrug.

Dad opened the letter and his eyes widened in disbelief. 'You'll never guess who this is from,' he said.

'Callum McCrumble,' we chorused.

'Is he offering to do the garden, plant trees or give us some new garden ornaments?' I asked.

'No,' said Dad. 'He's offering to lend me some money to fight Vladimir in court.'

'What!!!!'

'But only if I agree to sell the Crumbling Arms to him if I win. He says I could stay on as manager of the new tartan centre he would set up here, and that we could still live, as we do now, on the premises.'

'But . . . but . . . but he's been helping Vladimir, so why . . . ?'

'Perhaps Vladimir's pulled out of the deal. Perhaps that's why he's been going to see Callum at the big hotel. I've heard he's been there several times,' said Constable Ross. 'I think he really does want to live here and be clan chief.'

I looked at Dad. 'What are we going to do?' I said. 'We have to fight Vladimir, but we can't take any help, if that's what you'd call it, from Callum McCrumble. That's unthinkable.'

Dad gave a sigh that seemed to come from his soul. 'We may have to think the unthinkable, Kat. At the moment we have no choice. At least accepting Callum McCrumble's offer would keep me in a job and keep a roof over our heads.'

'But we can't do that,' I cried. 'I bet he made those offers to Kirsty and Morag and Donald to try to soften them up. To try to get them to persuade you to accept his money. But we just can't do that. There has to be another way.'

Trouble was, I had absolutely no idea where to find it.

Chapter 27

Henry McCrumble came round with his van later that day to collect the jumble for the Grand Jumble Sale. The sale was being held in the village hall the next day and I'd forgotten all about it.

'Sorry, Henry,' I said. 'I still haven't looked out anything much, but Kirsty has. She's left a box of produce and a box of jumble in the kitchen.'

Henry came through to the kitchen with me to collect it.

'How's Mrs Tiggywinkle?' I asked.

'Settled in no problem,' said Henry, 'and seems quite happy.'

'I wish I could say the same about us,' I sighed.

'I know,' said Henry. 'This Vladimir nonsense is

a bad business. Actually, Kat, I need to speak to your dad about something. Is he around?'

'Back yard,' I pointed, 'feeding Donk and Lily. I'll call him then I'll run upstairs and bring down my little pile of jumble.'

I opened the back door. 'Dad, Henry to see you.'

Dad put down the fresh bale of straw he was putting into Donk and Lily's little house and headed indoors. I ran upstairs to my bedroom. I looked hopefully into the jumble sale box to see if anything had mysteriously thrown itself in there in the night. It hadn't. There was still only a rather sad little pile of odd clothes. I had an idea. I picked up my pink fairy wand from the floor. 'Now's your chance to be of some use,' I told it, and closed my eyes. 'Empty box upon the floor, fill with jumble goods galore.' And I waved my fairy wand three times like they do in pantomime. I opened my eyes. Nothing had happened, funnily enough. Still, it had been worth a try.

'Right,' I said. 'That was your last chance, fairy wand. Into the box you go,' and I put it in on top of the clothes and carried the box downstairs.

Dad and Henry were deep in discussion at the kitchen table and didn't hear me arrive. A white envelope lay between them. Now, I suppose I could have minded my own business, and taken my box outside to Henry's van. Or, I suppose I could have minded my own business, and taken the dogs for a walk. Or, I suppose I could have minded my own business, and phoned Tina for a chat. But did I do any of that? Of course not. I stayed and listened. And what I heard brought a lump to my throat. Henry was trying to give Dad some money.

'It's not just my money, Hector,' I heard him say. 'It's come from everyone in the village. No one wants to see you and Kat put out of your home and the inn closed down. It's at the heart of the village. *You're* at the heart of the village. We don't want to see that change.'

'It's very good of you, Henry, to have organised this,' Dad's voice was a little bit shaky, 'but I can't possibly accept the money. There is no guarantee we will win the court case, then everyone would be out of pocket. Folks around here can't afford that. No, this is my problem and I have to solve it myself.'

And no matter how much Henry protested, Dad would have none of it.

He pushed the envelope gently back towards Henry. 'Please tell everyone how deeply grateful I am. How much I appreciate their kindness.'

I swallowed hard. Henry stood up and put the envelope back in his pocket. He picked up Kirsty's boxes and turned to go.

'Let me know if you change your mind, Hector,' he said. 'The offer is still there.'

Dad smiled but shook his head.

I followed Henry out to his van with my box.

'Your dad's a really nice man, Kat,' he said. 'But more stubborn than those donkeys in your back yard.'

I just nodded, not trusting myself to speak.

Henry climbed into his van. 'See you at the jumble sale tomorrow,' he said, and drove away.

I wandered back into the inn. Dad was already back out in the yard carrying on with his work. Max was helping by trying to nip bits of straw out of the bale. Millie had her nose on her paws watching him.

'I'm supposed to be helping at the jumble sale tomorrow,' I said to Dad. 'Is that OK? Tina and I are on the produce stall with Morag. She needs a hand. It's always very busy.'

'Of course it's all right, Kat,' said Dad. 'I'm going along tomorrow too. Mrs Corbet is donating an old piano and help will be needed to get it up the steps of the village hall. We're not too busy tomorrow so Kirsty and Donald can cope. So long as I'm around when Johnnie McAllister turns up. He's coming to fix the chimney tomorrow afternoon and might need some help.'

I nodded and went back indoors. The rest of that day passed in a dream. I know I helped serve the evening meals. I know I helped clear away the dishes. I know I was friendly and polite to the guests, but I was on automatic pilot, just going through the motions, my mind somehow not really connected to my body.

Later on, when the last guests had gone, I took my body to bed. I went through the nightly ritual of face washing, teeth cleaning, telling Max to get off my bed, and I slid under the duvet. I felt cold, a little numb. Even my hand with Millie's warm head resting on it seemed not to belong to me. I just lay there, for how long I don't know, till eventually I fell into a shallow, restless sleep.

Chapter 28

Next morning was busy. As soon as I had finished with the guests' breakfasts, I headed to the village hall. It lies two streets behind the Crumbling Arms and is used mostly for jumble sales, coffee mornings and ceilidhs. Every four or five years or so, it's used as a polling station. I'm not old enough to vote yet, but I will when the time comes. I like to have my say about things, as you know by now!

Inside the village hall it was chaos. The men were busy putting up trestle-tables and the women were frantically sorting through the jumble, trying to put it into orderly piles. All the men's clothing would be piled up on the tables on the left-hand side of the room, while the ladies' clothing would occupy the right. Across the top of the room, in front of the stage, were the tables for toys and produce. I tried not to look at the cuddly toys being set out. Kirsty would have a fit if I came home with any more.

Henry McCrumble's wife, Lottie, spotted me.

'Hi, Kat,' she said. 'I think this is to be your table here. Henry has put Kirsty's produce underneath along with the other contributions.'

'Thank you,' I said, and went to get some white paper to cover the paint-stained table. I was just cutting a large piece from the roll when Tina appeared, carrying a heavy box.

'Hi, Kat,' she said. 'Sorry I'm late, but Mum insisted I brought some of her home baking for the produce stall. What am I going to do with it? It'll never sell, unless anyone needs more stones for their rockery. But I didn't want to hurt her feelings by refusing.'

'Put it behind the stage curtains just for now,' I grinned, 'and we'll worry about it later.'

At least the jumble sale was giving me something else to think about. In the end, Tina and I had to have a table each, because people had handed in so much home-made jam, jelly and home baking that our one little stall overflowed.

'We'll still have to keep some of the produce

underneath,' said Morag, 'and just replenish the stalls when stuff gets sold.' Then she stiffened and looked at me strangely. Her eyes glazed over. The blue one took on its faraway look, and her voice sounded hollow and far away. 'I see strange happenings here,' she said. 'Strange happenings at the jumble sale . . .'

But before she could say more, her trance was interrupted by the arrival of Mrs Corbet's upright piano as the men from the village trundled it up a makeshift ramp and into the hall. The men were all red faced and puffing hard, including Dad. The piano was obviously very heavy. It was a handsome instrument, dark mahogany in colour, and inlaid with mother-of-pearl flowers. It sported brass candelabra on the front, where I suppose the candles would have gone in the days before electric light. I wondered fleetingly if people ever set their sheet music on fire, or if hot candle wax ever dripped down on to their hands as they played. If it had, piano practice could have been a dangerous business. The piano was immediately set upon by the Nisbet boys, who opened the lid and began to play. They really fancied themselves as hotshot musicians, but I have never heard 'Chopsticks' played so loudly or so badly before. Even when I had a go on the school piano, when the music teacher wasn't around, it didn't sound as bad as that. Honest.

Morag just shook herself out of her trance and carried on stacking up the pots of strawberry jam beside the jars of creamy lemon curd.

Amazingly, after a while, all the stalls were organised, and everything looked neat and tidy.

'Though that won't last long,' muttered Morag, 'once the hordes descend. Who on earth handed in that moth-eaten moose head? Imagine having that in your house.'

I stood back and surveyed our two tables. They were already bowing under the weight of the produce. I patted my pocket to make sure I had my pocket money with me to buy plenty of Kirsty's tablet.

'Kirsty's tablet!' I gasped to Morag and Tina. 'It's not here. It wasn't in the produce box Henry collected. Kirsty put it in a plastic box in the bottom of the fridge to make sure Max didn't get at it.'

'Better nip back quickly and get it then,' said Morag. 'Kirsty won't be too pleased if it doesn't get sold.'

'You've got time,' said Tina. 'There's still fifteen minutes till the doors officially open.'

I hurried towards the front door of the hall and slipped out. Already a long queue was forming outside. The Auchtertuie jumble sale was well known in the entire area as the place for good bargains. I wondered if anyone would buy my gorse-yellow shorts. I just hoped Morag wouldn't spot them on the clothing stall and be offended.

I ran all the way home. Kirsty was busy in the kitchen, and through the open back door I could see Donald and the dogs out in the back yard. Donald was attending to Jinty's chickens. Millie looked on interestedly as Donald added the last nails to the little chicken house. Max lay on his back with his paws in the air, getting a suntan. I liked the chickens. I'd got used to them being around, and would be quite sorry when they eventually went home.

Kirsty looked up and saw me. 'I thought you and your dad were helping at the jumble sale,' she said. 'Do the pair of you good to get away from here for a while.'

'We are helping,' I said. 'I've come for your tablet. I was just leaving it here till the last minute, so it would be fresh.'

Kirsty gave me a look. She wasn't fooled.

I grabbed the tablet from the bottom of the fridge and headed back out along the hall. Then I came to a sudden halt, and dropped the box. Old Hamish was hovering by the door of the lounge, just like he had been the other night.

'Hamish,' I breathed.

Hamish's long, sinewy hand stretched out towards me, then pointed to the lounge.

'The lounge,' I whispered. 'You want me to go into the lounge?'

In reply Hamish floated through the lounge doorway. Hardly daring to breathe, I followed him in.

'What is it?' I whispered. 'What are you trying to tell me?'

Hamish floated over to the fireplace. Again that long, sinewy hand stretched out towards me and the index finger beckoned.

I walked forward. 'What? I know there's trouble with the fireplace. Johnnie McAllister should be here at any moment to replace the fallen stones.'

Suddenly Old Hamish looked anxious and he pointed again. Not just at the fireplace this time, but, it seemed to me, actually up the chimney.

'The chimney,' I said. 'Is there something wrong with the chimney?'

Again he pointed. 'You want me to look up the chimney?'

Old Hamish nodded.

I hesitated. I knew, given the state of the chimney, that that could be dangerous. But I also knew that Old Hamish wouldn't ask me to do anything that wasn't absolutely necessary, so I decided to take a chance.

I opened the old log box and took out one of our emergency torches. Then I stepped into the fireplace, and looked at Old Hamish. He nodded. Feeling just a bit daft, I shone the torch up the chimney. Its beam picked out the rough old stones. I swung it round several times, but there was nothing there, just a faint little bit of sky showing through at the top.

'There's nothing here, Hamish,' I said, ducking out again.

But Old Hamish would have none of it. Again he agitatedly nodded his head. I picked up the little three-legged stool that sits by the hearth and stood on it. Again I shone the torch up the chimney. Still nothing ... no, wait. There was something, a loose stone, half knocked out from the fall. And there was something behind it, glinting in the torchlight. I put the torch down on the hearth, propped it up between two of the fallen stones and angled it towards the loose one in the chimney wall. Then I stepped back up on to the stool and reached up. A light fall of soot settled on me and made me gasp, but I could reach the stone. I strained upwards on tiptoe. I could just reach in behind it. My fingers touched something which felt like a metal clasp. I drew it towards me. What looked like a rectangular metal box came into view, as it scraped its way along the stone. I stretched upwards and forwards to grasp it and fell off the stool. I banged my right knee on the stonework as I went down, and ended up in a sitting position in the bottom of the fireplace, covered in soot. But I was clutching a rectangular metal box.

'Is this what you wanted me to find?' I asked Old Hamish. But I spoke to an empty room. Old Hamish had gone.

The metal clasp on the box had disintegrated with age so it was easy enough to unhinge it and look inside. I don't know what I expected. Gold nuggets or glowing jewels perhaps. Perhaps something we could sell to help save the inn. But it contained nothing like that. In fact it contained something much more precious. It contained a folded-up piece of parchment with some writing on the top. The writing was old and very spidery. I peered at it through sooty lashes. I wiped the soot from my eyes and peered again. The faint writing came into focus and I was sure I could just make out the faded words . . . 'Last Will and Testament of Hamish McCrumble'.

'Last Will and Testament of Hamish McCrumble,' I muttered. 'It's Old Hamish's father's will,' I cried. 'It has to be.'

Chapter 29

I jumped out of the fireplace, raced out of the lounge and into the kitchen.

'Kirsty! Kirsty!' I yelled. 'Look, it's what Dad's been searching for. It's Old Hamish's father's will, I'm sure of it. Old Hamish was here and showed me where to look.'

'What!' Kirsty dropped the carrot she was scraping and it rolled across the kitchen floor. Max immediately pounced on it.

Millie caught my mood and skipped around me excitedly.

'I'm off to tell Dad!' I cried. I knew I was still yelling, but I couldn't help it. I took off with Millie at my heels, leaving Max lying on the kitchen floor, happily crunching on the carrot now held upright between his two front paws.

I was so excited I barely noticed the odd looks I got as I flew along the village street. But, when I arrived, panting, at the village hall, I did notice the long queue waiting patiently outside. Waiting patiently to get inside to rummage among the jumble. They wouldn't be pleased if they thought I was sneaking in ahead of them.

'Back door, Millie,' I decided. 'Best go in through the kitchen.'

We hurried along the gravel path at the side of the hall, turned sharp right at the end and pushed open the bright blue back door. The kitchen helpers were busy making huge pots of tea and filling plates with home baking. They looked up in surprise when they saw me.

'Kat,' they exclaimed. 'Just look at the state of you! Why are you covered in . . . ?'

'Can't stop,' I gasped. 'Must find Dad right away.'

Millie and I burst into the hall through the door at the side of the stage and were immediately brought up short. The hall was noisy and packed full, and there was a slightly frenzied air as folks searched among the jumble for bargains. Frantically I scanned the crowd for Dad, but I couldn't see him anywhere. I saw the moose head being bought and carried aloft by the grinning Nisbet boys. Heaven knows what their mum would say when they got it home. I saw Tina and Morag, busy with a crowd of customers, all clamouring to buy bag loads of produce and home baking. I saw a clutch of interested people examining the old piano for woodworm and checking that all its keys still worked. But I still couldn't see Dad.

'He has to be here somewhere, Millie,' I said. 'Come on,' and I turned and ran up the steps at the side of the stage. 'We'll have a better view from up here.'

From my vantage point at the front of the stage, I scanned the sea of faces again. Henry was organising the people who wanted tea and cake into an orderly queue, and making sure they had their money ready. Luigi was arguing with another keen buyer over an almost new Harris tweed jacket, and I saw a woman buying my gorse-yellow shorts. I just hoped they weren't for her daughter. At last I saw Dad. At least I saw his old jeans and jersey appear from underneath a trestle-table. They were closely followed by the rest of him. Dad was holding a hammer, so I reckoned he'd been on his knees fixing a dodgy table leg. I jumped up and down, waved my hands in the air, and yelled,

'Dad!' But my voice was drowned out by a sudden commotion at the front door. Everyone turned to look as Vladimir, in full Highland dress, and accompanied by some of his tartan-trousered sailors, erupted into the hall. Vladimir certainly believed in making an entrance. I hadn't seen the tartan terrors outside, so they must have just arrived and jumped the queue, I thought. The angry faces, clearly visible through the open door behind them, said I was probably right. But Vladimir wasn't bothered. He was in clan chief mode.

'Good afternoon, my peoples,' he boomed. 'This is very good gathering here today. Very good indeed. But why you are not telling me about it? Why you are not asking me to it? When I am in charge I will open jumbly sale for you officially. Make little speech. Sit on big chair on platform and be clan chief, no?'

'No!' I yelled.

Everyone swivelled round and turned their attention to me.

'Kat!' said Dad, finally catching sight of me.

'I have something here that proves you're not the clan chief, Vladimir,' I said, and I held up the box containing the will. My hands were trembling and I knew my voice was too. And that wasn't all. A large centipede and his family seemed to be doing a tap-dance in my stomach, and my knees felt as though they belonged to a wobbly doll. Millie pressed in close to me in support.

'Kat,' said Dad, as he made his way through the crowd towards the stage. 'Kat, what is it?'

'I also am demanding to see what is it,' frowned Vladimir, and he too pushed his way forward. Vladimir's sailors looked at each other, shrugged and followed Vladimir. They were immediately followed by another group of men. The Auchtertuie warriors, organised by Henry, were ready for any trouble that might occur. They took up their stance behind the sailors. The atmosphere grew tense as silence fell and everyone stopped bargain-hunting to see what would happen.

'I found this in the chimney.' I held out the box to Dad. 'Old Hamish showed me where to look . . .'

Dad shook his head, took the box from my shaking fingers and opened it. Then he saw the contents. He saw the will with the faded spidery writing, and he gasped, his eyes widening in a mixture of relief and disbelief. 'Oh, Kat,' he finally said. 'Oh, Kat.' Carefully, he unfolded the old piece of parchment and read it. From the look on his face, I had no doubt it was what he'd been searching for.

Meanwhile Vladimir was getting impatient. 'What is this? What is this? I am clan chief. I demand to be told.'

'It's Old Hamish's father's will, Vladimir,' said Dad, 'and it proves that I am the rightful owner of the Crumbling Arms.'

'And the clan chief,' I added loudly, so everyone could hear.

Vladimir peered at the will. 'This could be a fake. A trick,' he blustered. 'You could have made this up, Hector McCrumble. You and that wild Kat of yours.' And he waved an imperious hand at me.

'We could have, but we didn't,' said Dad. 'We don't do that kind of thing. Anyway, we can let the lawyers decide. It won't take them very long.'

'Hmph.' Vladimir was not happy. He scowled as he turned to go. 'My claim is good. We shall see, Hector McCrumble. We shall see.'

'One more thing I think you should see, Vladimir,' said Dad. He went into the back pocket of his old jeans, took out a letter and handed it to him. 'I think you should read that carefully, and you might see something else too.'

I grinned. I didn't need my upside-down reading ability to know it was the letter Dad had received from Callum McCrumble. The letter that showed he was prepared to double-cross Vladimir. The letter that showed what a snake he was.

Vladimir's face darkened as he took in the contents. He thrust the letter back at Dad. 'Come,' he said to his sailors. 'There has been dirty work here. We go now to visit the big hotel. We have some other business to attend to.' And he strode off the stage to a mighty cheer and shouts of 'good riddance' from the crowd, who parted happily to speed his exit from the hall.

Dad turned to me and hugged me fiercely. 'Oh, Kat,' he said again. 'You did it. You saved us and the Crumbling Arms.' And the crowd cheered again as Henry McCrumble and the Auchtertuie warriors came up on to the stage and hoisted Dad and me shoulder high and paraded us round the room. There had never been a jumble sale like it. They were just putting us down again when Kirsty and Donald burst through the hall door.

'What's happened?' panted Kirsty. 'We came as fast as we could. We left Johnnie McAllister in charge of the inn. We saw Vladimir and his sailors march off up the street. Did we miss much? What's happened?'

I grinned and pointed at Dad. 'Why don't you

ask the newly confirmed owner of the Crumbling Arms and official clan chief,' I said.

And Dad grinned too. The biggest grin in the entire world or maybe even the universe.

Chapter 30

Everything got a bit surreal after that. The jumble sale flowed on round about us as people came to congratulate Dad and shake his hand. And mine. Dad told them all about my part in the discovery of the will, and where I had found the box.

'Who'd have thought it?' said Morag happily. 'But I knew something was going to happen at the jumble sale. Didn't I say so?'

'You did,' I said, and gave her a hug.

Then Dad went back to the inn to give Johnnie McAllister a hand, while I stayed to help clear up after the sale. 'I never did get to buy Kirsty's tablet,' I said to Tina and Morag, and told them about dropping the box. 'It'll all be broken now and we couldn't possibly have sold it.'

'Then we'll just have to eat the bits,' grinned Morag. 'Waste not, want not.'

'And it'll taste just as good,' said Tina.

'And it's no loss what a friend gets, Kirsty always says,' I grinned.

As usual, the sale did well, and Henry was very pleased with the amount that had been raised for the scanner for the cottage hospital. As usual too, all the cuddly toys had been sold, apart from one. It was a sad-looking Dalmatian, whose previous owner had taken a red felt-tip pen to him and tried to join all his dots. He looked so forlorn sitting there, that I just couldn't leave him. Don't know what I'll call him yet, though Jumble might not be a bad idea. Don't know what Kirsty will say when she finds out about him either, though I can probably guess.

When the clearing up was done, everyone came back to the Crumbling Arms. It seemed the natural thing to do, and no one seemed to mind the noise and the dust as Johnnie McAllister mixed up his cement and chipped away at the chimney stones in the lounge. Kirsty and Morag were kept busy making tea and buttering scones, and I had to tell everyone the story of finding Old Hamish's father's will over and over again. For a while it seemed like everyone was so pleased for Dad and me that they didn't want to go home. Finally, when no one could eat another morsel, they went away, and Dad and I were left alone.

I glanced at Dad. His face had lost the set, worried look he'd worn over the past weeks, and he appeared much younger, and much more like his old self.

'Don't know about you, Kat,' he smiled, as he locked up. 'I'm still exhilarated by today's events, but exhausted too.'

'It's been a funny old day,' I said, and hugged him fiercely and went to bed.

But that wasn't quite the last of the funny things that happened.

We heard, through Henry McCrumble's wife, Lottie's, second cousin, Sarah, that there had been a bit of a stushie up at the big hotel. Seems that Vladimir and his men had marched in, and, before anyone could stop them, had gone straight up to confront Callum McCrumble in his suite. Seems there were a lot of raised voices. Seems that Callum McCrumble phoned Constable Ross to come and eject the intruders, but unfortunately he was elsewhere on urgent business at the time. Seems that by the time he did get there, Callum McCrumble had already been carried down into the garden and thrown, fully clothed, into his own swimming-pool, in front of all the hotel guests.

Could that phone call have been the one Willie Ross got while he was helping Tina and Morag and me eat the unsold bag of empire biscuits on our stall? Who knows? Anyway, Callum McCrumble's gone now. Left in his helicopter, apparently not a happy man. He wouldn't be happy either when he got Dad's note, declining his offer of help to prove Dad's ownership of the Crumbling Arms. He wouldn't like Kirsty's note, or Morag's or Donald's either. I don't know what they said apart from 'no thank you'. I know what I would have said, but maybe the adults were more polite. Pity.

The other funny thing that happened was the disappearance of Vladimir's tartan boat from the loch, followed three days later by the arrival of a large parcel. Morag staggered in with it from her van.

'Well, what's this?' Dad smiled at her. 'Is it good news or bad?'

'Bad news that I've had to carry it in,' puffed Morag, 'but I'm not getting any nasty feelings from it, so good, I think.'

'Well, there's one way to find out,' said Kirsty, and handed Dad a large pair of kitchen scissors.

Dad cut through the thick brown tape securing

the box and opened it up. Inside were several pairs of McCrumble tartan trews and a full Highland dress outfit in the McCrumble tartan, including a black velvet tammie with a long grouse feather. There was no sign of a wig.

'That outfit has to be Vladimir's,' I said.

Dad looked at the accompanying note. 'It is,' he grinned. 'Apparently he has decided that my claim to the Crumbling Arms and to the chieftainship of the Clan McCrumble is probably better than his, so he has decided not to pursue it. He says he no longer has any need of the tartan outfits as he's decided to trace back his family tree on his mother's side. He seems to think he might be related to the Russian Czars.'

'Would you believe it?' said Morag. 'The man's a knockout.'

'Lunatic more like,' sniffed Kirsty.

'I think he just wants to belong somewhere,' said Dad.

'Och, you're far too nice about him, after all the trouble he caused you, Hector,' said Morag.

'And just what does he expect us to do with this box of tartan?' said Kirsty. 'I don't want it in here cluttering up my kitchen.'

'I'll take it,' I said immediately.

'You!' Everyone looked at me in surprise. 'Why?

Surely you don't want a souvenir of Vladimir?'

'It'll solve one of my major problems,' I grinned, as I picked it up and headed upstairs to my bedroom. 'Now I don't need to worry about collecting any jumble for next year's sale.'

Tooth-rotting recipe overleaf $\longrightarrow$

Recipe for Oatie Biscuits

These are really easy to make and are great for impressing ancient relatives who will think you're a genius.

6oz (150g) porridge oats
2oz (50g) self-raising wholemeal flour
2oz (50g) brown sugar
4oz (100g) margarine
1 teaspoon baking powder

- Mix everything together and knead for a few minutes (this can be squidgy and may remind you of making mud pies when you were little).
- Roll out on a floured board – the mixture, not you.
- Cut into rounds and space out on a greased tray.
- Bake in the oven at 350°F (180°C) for 15–20 minutes or until lightly browned.
- Put on a wire rack to cool.

Author's note: I sometimes substitute some chopped mixed nuts for a little of the porridge oats. Delicious, but only offer this version to ancient relatives who have all their own teeth.

KAT McCRUMBLE

Margaret Ryan

This is the first story about Kat McCrumble and her many pets.

Kat is happy helping her father run the Crumbling Arms. But trouble is brewing – the big hotel is trying to force them out of business, and worse still, badger baiters have been spotted nearby.

What can Kat do? Kat can get mad, that's what, and when that happens the world had better watch out! She hasn't got the McCrumble red hair for nothing . . .

By the winner of the Scottish Arts' Council Book Award.

SIMPLY KAT McCRUMBLE

Margaret Ryan

Another Auchtertuie adventure!

Kat's real passion is, of course, animals. She and her dad will look after anything, from donkeys to tarantulas.

Now they've given a home to their most unusual animal yet: a cute little wallaby called Wilf. He's a real character and soon has tourists flocking to see him. Then Wilf is kidnapped and Kat is furious. And when that happens, look out world!

OPERATION BOYFRIEND

Margaret Ryan

Abby can't wait for the arrival of her wild Grandma Aphrodite from Oz – and when they meet, she's not disappointed!

In her sheepskin coat, crocodile boots and sixties' clothes (not to mention that mysterious trunk – what could be inside it?), Aphrodite walks into Abby and her mum's life and turns it upside down.

Before long, they're dancing to The Beatles, bringing chaos to the neighbourhood, and hatching a brilliant plan to find Mum a man . . .

OPERATION HANDSOME

Nothing's been the same since Grandma Aphrodite came to stay from Australia. For starters, Abby's mum has finally found a boyfriend, and is acting like a teenager.

And now Grandma's husband, Handsome Harris, has disappeared. Could he *really* have been kidnapped by the Australian mafia?

One thing's for sure, Abby and her grandma will soon be hot on Handsome's trail . . .